365 Days of Becoming

A FICTIONAL MEMOIR BY
Julie Tomlinson

Published by Franklin Publishers
Printed in the United States of America
For permissions, inquiries, or additional copies, contact:
Franklin Publishers
www.franklinpublishers.com

Disclaimer

Any resemblance to real people, living or dead, is purely coincidental. While this novel may be inspired by real emotions and experiences, all characters and events are products of the author's imagination.

Dedication

For my seventh-grade English teacher, Mr. Donovan, who saw the potential in a quiet student and nurtured her spark, giving her the confidence to believe she could become an author.

Prologue

The pot of pasta bubbles over on the stove, sending starchy water hissing onto the burner. I lunge to turn down the heat, stretching out my leg to kick the refrigerator door shut. Multi-tasking is usually my strength, but tonight everything feels like a battle. Howie, my dog, whimpers at his empty bowl, waiting for his dinner, while the weight of another brutal work week presses down on me. Who knew public relations could be so exhausting? It's just media pitches and client meetings, for God's sake—yet somehow, it's relentless.

A vodka and Sprite sounds like the perfect remedy to take the edge off. I pour myself a double, the ice clinking as I fill the glass, and pull up my Taylor Swift playlist on Spotify. Just as the music starts, my phone buzzes. It's Quinn, my almost 10-year-old daughter sending me yet another YouTube video about acting and modeling agencies, right here in New York City, that she's eager to pursue. Recently, she's obsessed with the idea of "the big stage"—I can't help but want to shield her from the inevitable rejection she's bound to face. I sigh, relieved she's at her dad's this week. After all the late nights at work, I'm no one's idea of good company right now.

Leaning against the kitchen counter, I sip my drink, letting the familiar burn of vodka slide down my throat. My hand instinctively reaches for my phone, and before I know it, I'm scrolling through my dating apps. It's become a mindless ritual—standing here alone in my two-bedroom West Village apartment, waiting for my dinner to cook, swiping through faces in search of … something.

Dating apps have become my security blanket lately—how sad is that? I depend on them for a hit of affirmation, validation, and, let's be real, entertainment. Since coming out two years ago, I've been swiping left and right with a sort of hopeful resignation. A handful of decent women along the way, it's always the same story: I match with someone—and it's either ghost or be ghosted.

With the rarity of meeting people in the wild these days, I've come to appreciate the simplicity of dating apps—they make it easier for me to "put myself out there," something I've always struggled with. "Terribly shy," my mother labeled me from the beginning. Surprisingly, I've had decent luck. At 34, I've re-learned how to date, and trust me, dating women is no easier than dating men. In fact, it might be harder.

A wave of queasiness washes over me—my body feels hot, my head light. My mind urges me to keep swiping, to keep searching, but my heart is begging me to step back, to take a break from this endless pursuit of love. It's the kind of dilemma I should unpack with a therapist, but after developing an embarrassingly unhealthy crush on my last one, I promised myself I'd take a more personal approach to dealing with my crap.

A ping from an Ashley pops up. She's cute, but … Connecticut? That's way too far. I open a message from a Steph—her entire effort? "Hello." If that's all she's bringing to the table, I'm not wasting my time. There's Katie, a match in Brooklyn. But after scanning her profile again, I notice she doesn't want kids. Ugh, no thanks.

Disenchanted, I'm scrolling past all these beautiful women, but I'm tired of the game. Tired of the endless small talk, the shallow getting-to-know-you questions, the awkward first dates, the nervous anticipation of a kiss at the end of the night. Tired of the all-day texting that leads to a few months of good sex but, inevitably, ends in a heartbreak I should've seen coming. I've been through it enough times to know the truth: they weren't right for me from the start. Just notches on the ol' dating belt. And honestly? I'm done adding another notch.

Sitting cross-legged on the kitchen floor, I absently stroke Howie's fur, my mind lost in a haze of thoughts and emotions. My gaze drifts as I sink into a trance-like state, the weight of it all pressing down on me. I take a deep breath, closing my eyes just as Howie props his paws on my legs and licks my face, pulling me back to the present. And then, as if out of nowhere, it hits me—a profound realization.

Two years ago, after coming out as a lesbian and ending my marriage, I thought I'd finally get a fresh start—a chance to reclaim my life. But here I am, still stuck, still unhappy. The same bad habits cling to me, and I'm still just floating through life, waiting for it to feel like mine.

I'm too distracted—constantly caught up in everything around me, never pausing to listen to my own needs, confront my struggles, or nurture my soul. I spent my entire life suppressing my true self, becoming an unrelenting approval seeker. With every attempt to please others, I drifted further from my truth.

I think about all the superficial relationships I've entertained over the last couple of years—especially the last one, which was more of a situationship than anything real. I pause, wondering when I was last truly single. Embarrassingly, I realize I haven't been on my own since learning how to drive. From high school boyfriends to marrying Connor, to jumping headfirst into one lesbian relationship after another … it's been 18 years of never really being alone.

I push myself up off the kitchen floor, leaving Howie behind, and instinctively reach for my drink like it's a crutch. I take a few large sips, feeling the liquid courage slide down my throat. In this moment, I make a vow: one year off from dating. I've spent so long hiding behind relationships, using them as my ultimate distraction—when, in truth, I don't even know how to love myself yet.

It feels like a veil has been lifted, bringing a newfound sense of clarity. I grab my phone and open each dating app.

Account—Settings—Delete. One by one, they're gone.

My game plan is simple: get my shit together. For the first time in my life, I'm going to focus on me—really focus. It's time to reconcile my past and embrace the present, moving with purpose toward the future … in life, in love, in everything that matters.

After the year ends, I want to step into a version of myself I strive to become—stronger, clearer, and unapologetically myself.

CHAPTER 1
a big, fat dead end

It's been a week since I deleted my dating apps, and I'm finally starting to settle into this newfound freedom. No more endless swiping until midnight. No more obsessive tweaking of my profile. No more trying to figure out who's real and who's just another scammer. It's like a breath of fresh air I didn't know I needed.

The warm, breezy June night feels like the perfect evening for a long walk—a chance to let my mind go, and literally step away from the temptation of another night of drinking alone in my apartment.

Earbuds in, Pop2K on full volume, I weave through the maze of city dwellers and tourists like I'm on an obstacle course. As I glance up, I catch the sunset slipping through the narrow gaps between the buildings, and I can't help but admire the beauty of New York City kissed by the soft glow of the evening sun. In moments like this, I feel something—an inexplicable sense that maybe everything is connected, intertwined. Maybe it's the universe whispering that I'm exactly where I'm meant to be, perfectly in sync with this moment in time.

I'm excited—but nervous—about the year ahead. The perfectionist in me, the ultimate Type A overachiever, would dive into self-help books, download every meditation app and podcast out there, and diligently write in a gratitude journal each day. But this year, I'm deviating from what "typical Reilly" would do. Instead, I'm choosing a more reflective path—one that isn't mapped out by rigidness and structure—and other people's recipes on how to connect with your inner self. I'm letting my journey take me wherever it's supposed to go—a "fly-by-the-seat-of-your-pants" approach.

Since childhood, I've always stayed within the lines, coloring life neatly and predictably—out of anxiety, abandonment, and self-doubt. But now, without any guidelines, I'm hoping to take a deeper, more introspective look at myself. Maybe this way, I can finally confront my drinking problem, focus on being the best mother to Quinn, and nurture a stronger sense of self. Yes, this is my game plan—it's a game plan without a plan. It's terrifying, but I'm ready to see what happens.

A quick glance at my Apple Watch tells me I've been walking for over 45 minutes, and somehow, I've ended up in Midtown. Shit. Is this conscious or unconscious? Did I really just walk all this way, knowing Alexis lives here? I hope I don't run into her.

I turn down West 56th Street, and the unmistakable smell of Patsy's Pizzeria hits me—the best pizza in New York City, hands down. Since I'm here, I stop in for a slice. I grab a seat behind the street-facing window, intending to people-watch. But, as usual, I lose interest and get lost in my own thoughts. The last time I sat here at Patsy's was with Alexis—the last woman I "dated" (if we should even call it that) for nearly 10 months. I take a bite of my amazingly delicious pizza, letting the warmth of it melt on my tongue, but all I can taste is the memory of Alexis. Suddenly, it's not tonight anymore—it's last summer and we're in her bedroom—the place where you'd typically find us …

Alexis's one-bedroom apartment smells faintly of dryer sheets and nail polish, a mix that's oddly comforting. The only light comes from the soft, fluorescent glow of the white string lights hanging loosely along her wall, casting everything in a hazy warmth. Her hands graze my back, sending a ripple through me as every nerve ending comes alive. We kiss, soft and slow at first, our mouths barely touching. But as our breathing deepens, the kisses grow more urgent, the space between us disappearing with every moment.

With a playful grin, I grab Alexis by the arms and gently push her up against the wall, her legs instinctively wrapping around my waist. I peel her jean jacket off her shoulders, leaning in to nibble on her earlobe as my fingers weave through her thick, black hair. She's practically begging for it, and I waste no time slipping my hand down her pants, finding her wetness. Her moans start to fill the room—sweet, intoxicating sounds that fuel the fire between us. We can't keep our clothes on any longer, tearing them off in a frenzy. Woxers and red silk panties fly across the room as we fall deeper into each other.

On the bed, I take my time, kissing every inch of Alexis's smooth skin, starting with that sweet spot in the crook of her neck—the place she loves so much. My lips move slowly down her body, lingering over her voluptuous breasts, savoring the feel of her hard nipples beneath my tongue. I continue my journey, inch by inch until I reach her glistening pussy and begin to feast. My tongue slips deeply in and out, the pressure building, the pace quickening. Her moans fill the room, louder and more urgent, until she finally orgasms with me still between her thighs. Eureka. Now, her apartment smells like dryer sheets, nail polish ... and sex.

I lay there staring at the ceiling, feeling the weight of silence between us. This friends-with-benefits thing isn't working. We barely touch afterward— no cuddling, no connection—just a quick retreat to our own corners, like the whole thing was a transaction. The awkwardness hangs in the air, even as the music softly plays in the background. It's clear—we're just filling a need for each other, nothing more. I take a deep breath, knowing it's time to gather my things and call it a night.

As I lean back in the Uber, the bright, full moon lights up the sticky July night. My mind spins with random thoughts—shit, I forgot to pick up dog food ... I need to deposit that birthday check from Dad ... I'm out of ketchup ... I have that meeting at 8:30 am tomorrow. But then my mind drifts back to Alexis. Why doesn't she want to cuddle with me? Am I not good enough? Is that all I am to her—just good for sex? Why doesn't she actually want to be with me?

My chest tightens, a flash of insecurity rolling through me as if bracing for something inevitable. It's the same fear of abandonment I've battled for years, always lingering beneath the surface. And now, as a divorced, single mom, later-in-life lesbian, my biggest fear remains: ending up alone. This friends-with-benefits situation is only making it worse, feeding the flames of my anxiety. And the fire? It's leading me straight to a big, fat dead end. Why do I keep doing this to myself?

Don't get me wrong … I enjoy being with Alexis … a lot. The sex is good. No, it's great. And it's definitely creative. I'll never forget the time she followed me into the women's bathroom during the Backstreet Boys reunion concert, and we fucked to the sound of "Quit Playing Games with My Heart" blasting just beyond the bathroom doors. Or the time we had a staycation at The Hotel Chelsea, getting frisky in the hot tub for hours while hotel guests came and went as if nothing out of the ordinary was happening.

Lately, though, I've felt my feelings start to blur the line between friends-with-benefits and something more. I'm wanting to get closer … while Alexis, well, she's standing still. This is the risk I took when I agreed to a "no strings attached" relationship, but now I'm wondering—how could I ever be comfortable in something that's just for fun?

I want someone who actually … wants me.

I want the kind of relationship that is sweet, silly, flirtatious, and, most importantly, real. I want a partner who texts me songs that make her think of me … who looks at me in that one special way that makes my heart skip a beat … who reaches for my hand when we're driving … who cuddles with me after sex …

As the Uber pulls up to my stop, I peer out the window at my 16-story West Village apartment building. The streetlights cast a soft glow on the sidewalk, illuminating the few late-night strollers passing by. The car door swings open, and the softer sounds of the city greet me—distant chatter, the occasional honk, and the quiet hum of the neighborhood around me.

In my cozy plaid pajamas, candles flickering around the room, and a glass of wine in hand, I sink into the sofa and mindlessly scroll through the

TV. Friends—a reminder that I rarely see my own friends these days. Flip. Family Guy—I'm definitely not in the mood to compare Peter Griffin to the traits of my ex-husband tonight. Flip. Home Improvement—no thanks, I'm not ready for a trip down 90s nostalgia lane right now.

With a sigh, I switch off the TV and down the rest of my wine a little too quickly.

My apartment is quiet, still. The only sound breaking the silence is the steady tick-tock of a grandfather clock, an heirloom passed down from my grandparents. Absentmindedly, I start scrolling through photos on my phone, pausing on one of Alexis, covered in paint. That was the day we went to Paintball Authority in New Jersey … and ended up fucking in the backseat of her car on the way back to the city.

That same knotted feeling from the Uber returns, a tightening in my chest. Something's not right. When I picture Alexis, my anxiety shouldn't spike like this.

My phone buzzes. Of course, it's a text from Alexis.

(10:27 pm) Alexis:

Heyyy babe 😘

Thanks for 2nite.

Ur place or my place 2morrow nite?

I pause, my fingers hovering over the screen. One minute stretches into 10 as I wrestle with what to say. I should be honest, and tell her I'm not up for tomorrow. But instead, a few minutes later, I respond:

(10:38 pm) Riley:

My place.

The sharp clatter of a waitress dropping her pizza tray jolts me back to reality. I blink a few times, realizing I completely zoned out, lost in the memory of that night from a year ago.

Feeling full from the pizza—and weighed down by shame for staying in a dead-end relationship—I start the walk back to my apartment, my pace slower than when I'd arrived. After that night with Alexis, I kept playing the role of her beck-and-call girl for several more months … until I finally ended it. The breakup was awkward and uncomfortable—done via text message. *Typical Reilly.*

Back at my apartment, I flop down on the sofa, exhausted from all the walking and thinking. Howie hops up, settling himself across my lap, his warmth a small comfort against the churn of my emotions.

Maybe tonight was what I needed. I'd been a fool for too long, clinging to a relationship that was never meant to be more than it was. Has tonight finally given me the clarity to let go of Alexis?

I exhale slowly, the weight of the answer settling in. Yes …

Then why, despite everything, does she still linger in my mind? Why do I keep wondering what she's doing right now—who she's with, if she's thinking about me too?

I close my eyes, willing her out of my mind, but she remains, like a shadow I can't quite step out from under. The truth is, letting go isn't as simple as I'd hoped; her presence clings to me, quiet but unrelenting as if some part of me isn't ready to loosen its grip. Maybe Alexis still holds a piece of me, one I'm not sure I can—or even want to—release.

CHAPTER 2
connor

*O*utkast *blares from my iPod Shuffle speakers as my roommates prepare for their fourth night out in a row. It's Welcome Week at NYU, and while everyone else is buzzing with energy, I'm curled up in baggy sweatpants, glasses on, my hair an unbrushed mess since yesterday. It's 8:06 pm, and I've just popped some ramen noodles in the microwave before settling into our cheap IKEA futon, fully ready for a Laguna Beach marathon.*

The perfect anti-social evening is about to commence—until there's a knock at the door. Startled, I creep up slowly and peer through the peephole. Oh, it's that one guy from down the hall.

I open the door, and he smiles with a twinkle in his eye and a surprising amount of enthusiasm in his voice. "Hey, I'm Connor."

He glances at my PJ ensemble and laughs lightly. "Not planning to go out tonight?"

Suddenly, I feel like a complete dork for staying in on a Saturday night during my first week of college, but something about the way Connor says it makes me smile despite myself. What is he doing here?

After some small talk, awkwardly standing in the entryway to my dorm room, I start to understand why Connor is the go-to guy on Manchester Hall's fourth floor. After about 20 minutes of playful banter—debating who's better, the Yankees or the Mets, and which street vendor makes the best enchiladas—I decide he seems harmless enough … and I invite him in to watch some TV.

"I love hearing the story about how you and Daddy met," Quinn chimes, her smile brightening her whole face.

Sitting beside her on our balcony overlooking Bleecker Street, I take in the sound of her laughter mingling with the hum of the city below. These quiet, shared moments with her are like little treasures, slipping by too quickly but leaving a lasting sense of warmth.

A summertime thunderstorm is rolling in over the skyline, dark clouds gathering on the horizon. We call for Howie and head inside; it's time to start cooking dinner anyway. But as I chop vegetables for tonight's salad, my mind lingers on the memories of Connor, and the guilt I've carried with me from the start of our relationship.

From that Saturday night 16 years ago, when we stood in my doorway chatting about random shit, Connor and I became inseparable. We quickly moved from friends to something more, and soon, we were known as the "it couple" of Manchester Hall—college sweethearts who met in the co-ed dorms who were always up for a good time.

Connor wasn't just my boyfriend throughout college; he was my best friend. Sweet, charming, with a sense of humor that was one-of-a-kind. We could talk for hours at a time, hardly coming up for air.

But something inside me always felt off. When we touched, I didn't see fireworks or feel butterflies. Calling him any kind of pet name felt awkward on my tongue. Alone on the couch, cuddling wasn't my thing. In public, I never felt the urge to reach for his hand. And when we had sex, I didn't feel any kind of emotions—I was physically there, but mentally I was a thousand miles away.

That's because I'm gay. I always was. Deep, deep down, I knew it. I just didn't want to accept it. I'd been suppressing my attraction to girls since puberty, convincing myself that I wanted to "be" the girl rather than "be with" the girl.

In college, I met Connor within the first few weeks of my freshman year and, with him in my life, I could easily continue to suppress my true self—with the intention of fitting into society and seeking approval from my parents.

Connor was a wonderful distraction from the chaos I felt inside of me. From going to football games to partying at off-campus apartments to taking weekend float trips down the Hudson River, I got to live the heteronormative lifestyle (that I thought I wanted) and push down the anxiety within me that told me I was attracted to women.

To everyone else, Connor and I seemed like the perfect couple. But underneath the façade, I was straining every day to keep my secret buried. I convinced myself I was straight, that I was attracted to him. And even if I wasn't … I believed I could suppress those thoughts forever, take them to the grave, and no one would ever have to know.

Throughout our dating years, depression and anxiety clawed at me—usually during summer breaks when I went home and he did his internships. That's when my mind would spin out of control.

One night, just before my senior year of college, I woke up drenched in sweat from a dream that became my gay awakening. In the dream, I was intimate with a girl … and I liked it. I was shaken to my core. Everything I'd been suppressing suddenly made sense. I sat there in my bed at 3:00 am, paralyzed with fear, shame, guilt, and overwhelming sadness. It felt like my life was over. That night, as Mom, Dad, and my sister Raegan slept in their beds nearby, I contemplated suicide.

Somehow, I found enough fight in me not to follow through. But that summer, I cut myself off from the world, dropped to my lowest weight, and found my escape by zoning out to The Weather Channel for hours a day—watching shows about volcanoes, tornadoes, and other natural disasters, desperate to distract myself from the storm inside me.

Back at college for my final year, things picked up right where they left off with Connor and me—college sweethearts reunited. I never told Connor about my dream. And in my mind, I labeled myself bisexual—much easier to live with than gay. And I still wouldn't have to tell anybody. Life could go on like normal.

After college, our lives together unfolded like a storybook. Connor proposed to me on a beach in Miami. We moved into an industrial-style apartment in Brooklyn. Our careers took off. And at 23 years old, we got married on a beautiful summer day in the backyard of my parent's home, surrounded by family and friends, basking in their love.

For so long, I tried to convince myself that what we had together was enough for me. But it wasn't. Looking back, I truly loved Connor—just not in the way you're supposed to love someone when you marry and spend your life with them. I loved him as a friend, deeply, but I never love-loved him. Not the way he deserved. Not the way he loved me.

I still carry this guilt with me today. Guilt for using our relationship as a shield, for pretending to be someone I could never truly be. Guilt for keeping up the façade of a "good" marriage for eight years, only to watch it crumble into pieces.

I glance from the kitchen into the living room, spotting Quinn gently petting Howie. Another episode of *Family Feud* is playing on The Game Show Network—our favorite show to watch together during dinner.

I've come a long way since that shy, insecure freshman in college, always afraid of being seen. Maybe it's time to stop dwelling on the guilt. Why should I feel guilty for finally honoring my true self?

CHAPTER 3
the skylark building

It's barely 8:30 am, and the August heat is stifling. I duck into the Starbucks a block from my workplace, squeezing my way into the line, careful not to let my work bag bump into the hordes of people hustling to start their day. I glance at my watch. 8:06 am. Well, I'll only be a little late today. When I finally reach the counter, I order my usual—avocado toast and a venti cold brew with two pumps of white chocolate mocha, four pumps of sugar-free vanilla, and a splash of heavy cream.

With my breakfast and coffee in hand, I trudge up to the Skylark Building on Seventh Avenue in the Garment District and slip into the elevators. As I wait for the doors to close, I spot Madison—the gorgeous security guard who works the day shift at the front desk.

I wish I had the courage to flash her a playful smile and wink at her before the elevator doors shut, but I'm too timid.

Working as the Director of Public Relations at J/PR is a double-edged sword. The job is a whirlwind of late nights, tight deadlines, and demanding clients ... but it also comes with its fair share of perks—front-row concert tickets, access to exclusive parties, and priority seating at NYC's newest clubs. But the perks are getting old, and the stress is becoming all-consuming.

Straight out of college, I landed a lead coordinator role at one of NYC's most established PR firms. I quickly made a name for myself … though, looking back, it was mostly because I was a people-pleasing workaholic. I liked to think my early success was driven by a passion for the work, but in reality, much like my masked relationship with Connor, I used my career to hide the deep anxiety I felt about my sexuality. Still, years away from coming out, the deeper I buried myself in work, the less pressure I felt to confront the lie I was living in my personal life.

When I was recruited by J/PR, I quickly climbed the proverbial corporate ladder. And here I am today—worn down by a career spent managing the reputations of greedy corporate giants who manipulate consumers into buying yet another product or service they don't need.

I settle into my office and glance out the window at the busy streets below. My mind wanders back to Madison downstairs in the lobby. Tall legs, long, wavy blonde hair, and that irresistibly cute smirk. My thoughts drift into a mesmerizing daydream—imagining all the sexy things I'd love to do with her on that security desk.

Xandra, my ever-efficient communications assistant, pops into my office, snapping me back to reality. "Good morning, Reilly!" she says brightly. "Did you see the meeting scheduled for 11:00 am? I can prepare a status report if that would be helpful."

I nod, appreciating her initiative. "Yes, Xandra, that'd be excellent. Thank you."

Just then, my phone dings, pulling me abruptly out of my thoughts. I glance at the screen, half convinced I'm seeing things. But no—there it is. A text from Alexis. Seriously?

(8:52 am) Alexis:

Hi. How R U doing?

I stare at the phone for a solid minute, confused. My brain is racing. Why the fuck is she texting me? We haven't spoken in months.

Back in the spring, I ended things. Saying it was hard doesn't even begin to cover it. I felt a whirlwind of emotions, but more than anything, I felt like I let her down. How insecure is that? To Alexis, it must have seemed so abrupt, and honestly, breaking up over text was childish. Neither of us got the closure we deserved.

I can't deal with this right now. I shove my phone into the desk drawer, determined to block it out for the rest of the day. Whatever game Alexis is playing can wait until after work.

It's 6:30 pm and I pick up Quinn from her friend's apartment a few blocks from our place. The unease from Alexis's surprise text still lingers, gnawing at me all day. I know I have to respond, and the thought of it makes me anxious. I keep overthinking the tone of voice I want to use. I don't want to seem excited to hear from her … because I'm not. But I also don't want to come across as sad, like I miss her … because I don't.

Ugh.

Stop analyzing it and just fucking respond, Reilly.

(7:22 pm) Reilly:
Hi. I'm well. How are you?

There, that wasn't so hard. But now, the volley kicks off.

(7:24 pm) Alexis:
Not good. My mom passed away.

(7:25 pm) Reilly:
Oh my God, I am so, so sorry. 🙏

(7:26 pm) Alexis:
Thank u. The chemo stopped working last month. I knew it was coming, but … it's still so hard. I needed to tell u.

My current thought … I'm an asshole. I should have responded earlier in the day. I'm shocked she felt compelled to reach out to me, of all people. I mean, I know what it's like to lose a parent, but we're not girlfriends anymore … I mean, friends … I mean, fuck buddies. So what now? Should I offer to come see her?

(7:28 pm) Alexis:

Services are going to be Friday. I was wondering if u can come.

I open a bottle of wine as I process Alexis's ask. Tonight, I'm definitely drinking. Perhaps she's so grief-stricken that she's losing it and making really regrettable decisions right now. With some contemplation and apprehension, I respond a bit later.

(8:06 pm) Reilly:

Yes, I'll be there.

I curiously notice the timestamp of the text—8:06. Weird. I always see that number.

The next morning, the blare of my alarm snaps me out of sleep, and Howie, ever punctual, leaps off the bed, scampering toward his food bowl like clockwork. I groan, my mind still tangled in last night's conversation with Alexis, the remnants of an entire bottle of wine clouding my thoughts. It's a familiar haze—one that has been present since my early twenties when drinking became less of an indulgence and more of a habit.

We had talked until 11:15 pm, skimming the surface with safe topics—new Broadway shows, the city's best tapas spots. Nothing too deep, nothing too revealing. But then, unexpectedly, I told her about my year-long hiatus from dating, my commitment to personal growth—and finding myself. Her response was instant and genuinely supportive.

"Mom, come check out this YouTube video!" Quinn says, her words muffled by a mouthful of cereal as she sits at the kitchen table before school.

"Quinny, honey, I'm not watching another modeling agency video right now," I reply, my tone a little sharper than intended as my hangover headache starts to throb.

Quinn reacts immediately. "No, Mom! It's a funny video about kittens."

I feel a pang of guilt. Don't assume, Reilly. I step over to stand beside her, leaning in to watch the minute-long clip of kittens tumbling over each other. Quinn beams as I laugh along with her, and for that small moment, it feels good—like I've given her exactly what she needed.

As I prepare Howie's breakfast and tidy up the kitchen, fragments of a dream from last night suddenly flood back. It hits me all at once—wow, it was a steamy dream. Wiping the countertops, I try to piece it together. There was an office building. Another woman. We were alone. And we had sex … Slowly, the pieces lock into place, and I freeze. My heart skips a beat. It wasn't just any woman … it was Madison. No, wait … not Madison … Alexis!

Holy shit.

Wait … wait … does this mean anything? I try to rationalize it away in my head. Madison was on my mind yesterday, and then I talked to Alexis—it's just a coincidence, nothing more. Just a mash-up of encounters creating a wild, steamy rendezvous. My memory still fuzzy, here's what I can recall …

It's after hours, and the Skylark Building is deserted, save for the janitorial staff who always start from the top floors and work their way down. The lights are dimmed, the front entrance is locked, and a heavy, expectant silence fills the air.

Alexis sits seductively in an office chair, her legs crossed, a teasing smile playing on her lips as she toys with a pen, slipping it between her teeth. The scent of her perfume—a delicious, intoxicating blend—pulls me closer. I lean over, catching Alexis's gaze as I nudge her legs apart with my knee. Our lips meet in a fervent kiss, and I can feel her body responding. My fingers work the buttons of her blouse, revealing her breasts framed in a delicate red lace bra.

Desire takes over. I guide her onto the desk, tugging her pants down over her long, sculpted legs, every move heightening the tension between us.

My hands trace the curves of her body, my own desire throbbing inside me. With a quick snap, her bra falls away, and I lower my mouth to her breasts, sucking and teasing, reveling in their softness.

Gently, I let my fingers explore, feeling the heat through her soaked panties. I slide the fabric aside, slipping my fingers inside her, moving slowly at first, building the rhythm. Alexis's moans grow louder, more urgent until they turn into cries of pleasure. Her body quakes, pulsing around my fingers as she comes, the intensity radiating through her.

As the tremors subside, I bring my fingers to my mouth, savoring the taste of her, letting the moment linger in the charged air between us.

As I unload the dishwasher, a smirk tugs at the corner of my lips, the vividness of last night's dream still clinging to me like a heady, intoxicating haze. Maybe it's a stretch, but I can't shake the feeling that this wasn't just some fleeting fantasy, drifting in and out of my mind without purpose. What if it was something more—a whisper from the universe, a subtle reminder that Alexis is still woven into my life's tapestry in ways I can't fully grasp yet?

Maybe, just maybe, she dreams of me, too. Maybe there's unfinished business between us, a tether pulling us back together, some unspoken force binding us in ways that reach beyond logic. Alexis keeps resurfacing in my life, a thread weaving itself through something unfinished—something that tugs at the edges of my soul, refusing to let go.

CHAPTER 4
hypocrite

*D*r. Woodland pops his head in, a grin plastered across his face as if this is just another casual Tuesday. "Let's get this party started, shall we?" His voice is too chipper, too light, for the sheer agony of the contractions ripping through my body. I glare at him, my jaw tightening as a sharp retort simmers just beneath the surface. Of course, I say nothing. Party? I wouldn't call childbirth a party. I can feel my sanity fraying at the edges.

With the epidural finally kicking in, I adjust myself in the hospital bed, searching for some semblance of comfort amidst the wires and tubes. My body relaxes, but my mind doesn't.

Connor sits next to me, his face illuminated by the glow of his phone as his thumbs move swiftly across the screen. He looks … proud. Enormously proud. This soon-to-be father, texting away, probably letting his buddies know that the big moment is close.

I glance out the snow-frosted window, feeling the coolness of the scene outside contrasted by the warmth of this hospital room, where so much is about to change. A tear slips down my cheek before I can stop it. I'm excited to bring this baby girl into the world. But underneath that excitement is a layer of terror that I can't seem to shake.

While Connor is probably imagining perfect family moments—me holding our daughter for the first time, the baby falling asleep on his chest, walks to the park in the springtime—I can't seem to focus on any of that. Instead, my mind spirals into the one thing I can't escape: this baby, our baby, binds Connor and me together. Forever.

And with that realization comes the resurgence of all the thoughts I've spent years burying away. I made the right decision to marry Connor, didn't I? He's the best thing that's ever happened to me, right? I'm attracted to him … aren't I? Actually, no, Reilly … you're fucking gay. Oh my God, I just said it out loud in my head. No, you're just bisexual. And no one will ever need to find out.

Panic toils through me, twisting in my chest and making it hard to breathe. It's that same familiar turmoil, the kind that's haunted me for years. This is crazy. Our beautiful baby girl is about to enter the world, and yet I'm selfishly distracted by the chaos of emotions and secrets I swore I'd keep locked away.

My blood pressure spikes, prompting the nurses to rush in and check on me. I offer a shaky reassurance, telling them it's just anxiety and that I'll be fine. One of the nurses frowns, her voice calm but firm. She says if it happens again, they may need to administer something to help me relax. They can't let this interfere with the delivery.

I remind myself—for the millionth time—that I chose this life. The straight life. I could have taken a detour somewhere along the way and explored a different path, but I never took the off-ramp. I never allowed myself to wonder what might be on the other side. And now … now it's far too late. I'm about to have Connor's baby. There's no U-turn allowed.

To calm myself, I cling to the one image that makes sense: I want nothing more than for our baby to grow up with a mother and a father. A happy, "normal" family unit. The way it's supposed to be. The way I had it growing up. She will have it, too.

On December 19th at 1:36 pm, Quinn Kennedy Berkeley enters the world. Dr. Woodland lifts her up with a gentle pride, much like the presentation of Simba in The Lion King, *and in that instant, our eyes meet. Bright blue, piercing, and full of wonder—Quinn stares back at me with* an intensity that takes my breath away. It's as if she's already tuned into me, already sensing the depths of my soul, trying to understand who I am, like we share an unspoken connection beyond words.

The nurses move swiftly, cleaning her off and wrapping her snugly in a soft blanket before placing her in my arms for the first time. As Quinn nestles herself into the crook of my arm, a tenderness floods through me, and I realize my life has irrevocably changed. I'm a mother now.

The tumultuous thoughts that consumed me earlier in the day have faded into the background. All that matters now is the tiny life cradled in my arms. An overwhelming force surges within me, fierce and protective. At this moment, I know without hesitation—I would die for her.

Time is already moving too fast. I look at the clock and it's 8:06 pm. The day has been filled with visits from adoring family and friends, all eager to glimpse Quinn Kennedy—the perfect product of a seemingly perfect couple. She rests quietly in her bassinet just a few feet away, oblivious to the whirlwind of love that surrounds her. I'm exhausted from the day's excitement, every emotion pulling me in different directions.

I take a small, reluctant bite of the Jell-O in front of me. My appetite is nonexistent, but the nurses are relentless, insisting I eat every few hours to keep my energy up for breastfeeding. The room has finally settled into a comforting stillness. Connor is off somewhere, likely hunting down a cup of coffee. I glance out the frosted window again and find the full moon glowing brightly against the winter sky.

In this quiet moment, a vivid vision unfurls before me—the next 10 years of our lives, painted in snapshots of joy. I see Quinn crawling for the first time, then her first wobbly steps. I see her playing t-ball, then the day we pick out a puppy from the Humane Society. I imagine Christmas Eve, baking cookies together, school supply shopping for her perfect Nike backpack, and a magical family vacation at Disney World. So many smiles. So many memories.

But beyond that gleaming façade of happy times, another image persists—an image of me, deeply unhappy. Quinn will likely grow up with a sad, alcoholic mother who has lived her life in fear instead of truthfulness. My heart sinks.

I slowly edge myself off the bed, careful not to disturb the quiet, and step over to Quinn's bassinet. Watching her tiny chest rise and fall, her face peaceful in sleep, the words come to me effortlessly. "My one mission as your mother, Quinny-girl, is to raise you in a world where you feel free—always free—to be exactly who you are, your true, beautiful self."

Well, there it is—right from the start of my journey into motherhood, I'm promising Quinn the kind of life I've never honored for myself.

I am. Officially. The world's. Biggest. Hypocrite.

"Did you find everything you were looking for today?" the chipper Target cashier asks, her voice snapping me out of my flashback. I can't believe this memory found me—right here, in the middle of the checkout line—as my orange juice, Clorox, and fabric softener get scanned.

Back home, I unpack the groceries while a rerun of *Friends* hums in the background. It's the episode where Ross finds out Carol is a lesbian. What a coincidence. I let my mind wander to the life I might've had if I never would have come out.

Sometimes, I lie awake at night, wondering if Quinn has truly accepted me for who I am. I want to believe it—need to believe it—yet a small, gnawing doubt whispers to me in the darkness. Maybe she's too young to fully understand it all. Maybe she's just pretending to accept the divorce and my sexuality because it's easier than facing the conversation.

I don't know.

What I do know is that my mission as her mom hasn't changed since the night she was born, when I gazed at her peaceful little face and made a promise to raise her to be her genuine, authentic self. Well, mostly—as for acting and modeling?

That's where I draw the line.

CHAPTER 5
the conversation

Like any proud mom, I sit on the cold, hard bleachers, my eyes glued to Quinn as she commands the basketball court. Every movement is fluid and confident—she's easily one of the best players on the Basketball Stars of New York travel team. Even at her age, she's a natural leader, always lifting up her teammates with encouraging words and offering a steady, calming presence. I hope she continues playing basketball instead of giving it up to chase her latest obsession of show business. She's an athlete, not an entertainer. Or so I'd like to think.

As I watch Quinn on the court, so focused and determined, I can't help but wonder if some part of her has always been like this, through lifetimes we can't even remember. Recently, I've been introduced to the idea of past lives, and it's stirred something in me. I find myself imagining who Quinn might have been—a healer, a warrior, maybe even a queen from some forgotten era. Lately, I've been consumed by these thoughts, trying to connect the dots between who we are and why we do the things we do. What if our lives are just chapters in a much larger story? Questions swirl in my mind, always at the forefront: What is life, really? What lies beyond death? Is there something more—are we part of some grand design, or are we all just passing through, waiting to begin again?

Now that I finally have the space to focus on myself, I'm drawn to unravel the mysteries of life and whatever awaits on the other side. This curiosity feels like a current, pulling me deeper into the unknown—and I'm ready to follow wherever it leads.

Quinn dribbles down the court, fakes a pass, and takes a clean jump shot. Swoosh. The opposing coach quickly calls a timeout as Quinn and her teammates head to the bench for water. Coach Hillerson gives Quinn a high-five, and as she looks over her shoulder, her eyes find me and Connor sitting in the stands.

Connor sits beside me, though there's a noticeable gap between us, one I'm sure hasn't gone unnoticed by the other parents. I wonder if they know we're divorced. Despite the space, we're mostly amicable. Most of our conversations revolve around Quinn—her activities, school, and friends—but every now and then, we'll catch up on each other's families, work, and the usual small talk. What matters most is that when Quinn scans the crowd, she sees both her parents there, together, supporting her. No drama. No bullshit.

As the second quarter winds down toward halftime, Connor suddenly turns to me. "Anna's about to get here," he says casually. I blink, caught off guard. Anna? Who the hell is Anna?

Connor fills in the blanks quickly—apparently, Anna is his latest, and very serious, girlfriend. They've been dating for six months. Met in some single parents' group on Facebook, of all places.

I force a congratulatory smile. I am happy for Connor—at least, I think I am. Yes, of course, I am. How could I not be? He deserves love, deserves to be with someone who can love him fully in ways I never could. So why does the thought of meeting Anna make me feel so strange?

Maybe it's because, deep down, I'm already imagining the day Connor's new girlfriend becomes Connor's new wife. And then … Quinn gets a bonus Mom. And that idea terrifies me more than I'd like to admit.

Before I can stop it piercing through my mind, a vivid memory jolts me back to that night—the conversation that changed everything.

The night air is misty, and a gentle breeze sweeps across our Brooklyn balcony as Connor and I sit together, sipping hot chocolate spiked with Fireball. It's a quiet Friday night, the kind that used to bring comfort, but tonight, I can hardly focus. Connor leans back, a bit of swagger in his posture as he puffs on a Cuban cigar, while I do my best to avoid the swirling smoke. Quinn is sound asleep in her room, oblivious to the storm rolling in between her parents. I bite nervously at my fingers, barely able to believe that I'm about to shatter the world Connor and I have created.

These last seven years of marriage have been the hardest of my life. Each day has felt like a battlefield in my mind—a constant struggle between the undeniable attraction I feel toward women and the desire to hold on to the life I've built with Connor.

Tonight, I'm ready to face my truth—but only part of it. I'm going to tell him I'm bisexual. It's a step toward being more authentic, both for myself and for Quinn. As for the relentless, nagging curiosity about exploring my sexuality with women … it's become so consuming that I can't ignore it any longer.

I glance over at Connor, so blissfully unaware of the bombshell I'm about to drop. Okay, Reilly. Just do it. Now or never. My voice cracks as I ask him to listen—really listen—before saying anything. He nods, oblivious to the gravity of what's coming.

For the next four and half minutes, I talk. I tell him that I'm bisexual—careful of my words not to say too much by accident. His face remains blank, his eyes distant, as if he's processing it in slow motion. So far, his reaction is pretty much what I expected—silent, unreadable. The seconds stretch out like an eternity.

Finally, Connor speaks. "Cool."

Wait. What? Cool? Did he hear me? Did he miss the whole "bisexual" part?

Connor's expression shifts—almost excited, even a bit ... giddy?

"I want you to embrace who you are," he says, his voice light. "I support you. I want you to explore this side of yourself ... "

There's a pause. I brace myself, sensing the weight of what's coming next.

"... as long as it still involves me," Connor finishes, his tone steady.

Dumbfounded, I find myself now staring back at Connor with a similar blank gaze. This is definitely not how I imagined the conversation would go. Connor is thinking about threesomes.

My brain feels like it's short-circuiting. I take a few deep breaths, trying to steady myself. The people-pleaser in me begins to take over, whispering that maybe this is the perfect solution. It lets me explore my sexuality while keeping our marriage intact. A win-win, right?

Connor looks chipper, even smug like he's just won some kind of prize. A few minutes ago, he had no idea what kind of truth I was about to reveal, and now he's sitting here, feeling like the king of the hill. But I—I'm uneasy. Deeply uneasy. This doesn't feel right. It's not about casual hookups or threesomes for me. That's not what I want.

I want to explore my attraction to women, yes—but I want more than just sex. I want to date women, to experience that connection. I want to feel a woman's soft touch, to hold her hand, to bask in the warmth of her embrace.

I reassure Connor that I'm not going anywhere and that I'm committed to us, but I also need him to understand this isn't just about sex. It's more than that—so much more.

"Connor, have you heard of polyamory?" I ask, cautiously.

"No, but I've heard of polygamy," he replies with a slight smirk.

"No, not quite," I say, shaking my head. "Polyamory is the practice of being in a romantic relationship with more than one partner at the same time—with the informed consent of everyone involved. In simpler terms ... a throuple."

Connor looks stunned. Two women at the same time? All the time? Yeah, this probably isn't the dream scenario he imagined. But then again, it does mean all the threesomes he wants. I play that angle up a little.

To my surprise, Connor's on board.

But am I? Is this really what I envisioned when I pictured myself as a queer woman? Married to a man, in a polyamorous relationship?

It doesn't feel like the freedom I was hoping for.

Grinning from ear to ear, Connor stands and leans over, planting a kiss on my forehead. He declares that this is the start of a new chapter for Reilly and Connor. I force a smile in return, once again giving an Academy Award-worthy performance, suppressing the true whirlwind of emotions and desires that churn beneath the surface.

We raise our mugs of hot chocolate and Fireball, clinking them together in a toast.

"To becoming a throuple!" Connor resounds.

The referee blows the whistle; the fourth quarter is about to start. Connor returns to the bleachers with Anna by his side and introduces us. It's only slightly awkward, the kind of awkwardness that clings to the edges of politeness. I manage a friendly hello, but inside, I can't help but wonder if she's silently judging me. Judging me for being the one who ultimately walked away from Connor, for relinquishing the ultimate lie I carried for so long. Whatever issues they'll have together—emotional baggage, trust issues—she'll probably blame me for them all.

Stop it, Reilly, I tell myself—shaking off the absurd thoughts. I turn my attention back to the game. Just 15 more minutes and Quinn and I can head to Polar Paradise for snow cones, our post-game ritual.

Quinn hits a two-point jumper, tying the game 22-22. Connor jumps to his feet, cheering, and when he sits back down, he high-fives Anna before turning to offer me one as well. I take in the moment— Connor and I have come a long way since the night everything changed.

Suddenly, Quinn steals the ball, racing down the court on a breakaway. With effortless grace, she lays it up and beams back at us, her smile wide and radiant, eyes sparkling with pride. She sees me, her dad, and Anna—each of us there, together, watching her. It's a strange, new reality, but in this moment, it doesn't feel so foreign. It feels … possible.

Maybe this is what a blended family could look like one day—something that, with time, could fit together in its own imperfect way. Am I too hopeful?

For now, I'll hold onto this point in time and surrender to the flow of the universe, trusting that it will guide us all—Connor, Anna, Quinn, and me—toward the family we're meant to become … together or separate. Sometimes, letting go and trusting in the journey ahead is all we can do. And right now, it feels like enough.

CHAPTER **6**
the unicorn

The silky hotel sheets are bunched at the edge of the bed, the luxurious duvet is tossed carelessly on the floor. Our naked bodies intertwine as we kiss and grind against each other. Slowly, I roll on top of Olivia, pinning her beneath me, my hands tracing the soft curves of her body.

Being with a woman feels like discovering an entirely new language—every touch is a whisper, every curve a masterpiece, every kiss a delicate promise.

Olivia's soft moans fill the air each time my lips graze her neck just below the ear. I can't tell if I'm awake or dreaming—it's all a haze of sensation and warmth. She nibbles at my earlobe, and I lose myself further, completely captivated by the softness of her skin and the electric connection between us. Before I know it, Olivia rolls us over, taking control. She slowly moves her way down my body and slips two fingers inside me. Her movements are slow and deliberate, massaging me as her lips descend between my legs. She flicks her tongue against my clit, her fingers working rhythmically, too. I moan louder than I realize, certain the hotel neighbors can hear.

I'm completely lost in the ecstasy of Olivia's touch.

Until I remember—Connor is in the room, too.

Howie tugs at his leash with all his strength, thrusting me back to the present moment—his eyes locked on a squirrel darting up the snow-covered tree trunk. It's only October, and New York City has already had its first snowfall. People all along Bleecker Street are digging their cars out of the snow and chatting with their neighbors about how global warming is really a thing.

The air's coldness bites at my cheeks, and I silently urge Howie to hurry up and do his business so we can retreat to the comfort of our apartment. Today I took a mental health day—no work, no stress. Once Quinn is off to school, I plan to curl up with a steaming cup of lavender chamomile tea and dive into my new lesbian romance novel.

But Olivia is on my mind. As Howie and I turn to head back down the street, the snow begins to fall lightly again, soft flakes drifting across my face. My thoughts wander with them, floating back into the past, carried away on the cold breeze.

Four months into our throuple experiment, Connor and I were thrilled to have met Olivia. She was an aspiring songwriter with a magnetic presence—full of spunk and charisma, with just the right touch of quirky that kept us wanting more, especially me.

We found Olivia on a dating app designed for couples looking to add a "unicorn" to their relationship—someone who could seamlessly fit into the dynamic of an established couple and date both partners. Dating her with Connor was both thrilling and awkward. Thrilling, because I was finally dating a woman. Awkward, because it meant sharing that experience with my husband.

Olivia was a pro. It wasn't her first polyamorous relationship, and she took my inexperience with grace and patience. When I asked her why she wanted to be a unicorn, she smiled and said, "Why can't I have my cake and eat it, too?"

The truth is, I wanted Olivia to myself. I wanted to text her without involving Connor and go on dinner dates with her … alone. I wanted to have sex with her … just the two of us, without Connor in the room. My relationship with him started to shift, and I could tell he sensed it.

The deeper I dove into this exploration of bisexuality and polyamory, the clearer it became—stop pretending to be bi … you're fully gay. I didn't find Connor, or any man for that matter, sexually attractive. And, reflecting back, I never did. The emotions I felt when I was with Olivia didn't even come close to what I felt when I was with Connor.

The cold, hard truth started to stare me down, day in and day out. I numbed myself each night with a bottle and a half of wine, hoping to drown out the feelings that felt impossible to ignore.

One cold, snowy day just before Christmas, Olivia and I decided to play hooky from work. Despite the weather, the nearby wine bar called our names, so we bundled up and trudged down the street to Vin Sur Vingt. After finishing our first bottle of Margaux, we ordered a second, our laughter growing louder as we playfully flirted. I loved every minute of it.

The wine loosened my nerves, and before I knew it, I felt more open than I ever had been. Without planning to, I confided in Olivia. I told her that I didn't want to be in a polyamorous relationship involving Connor anymore. I wanted to end my marriage. And then the words spilled out: I'm not bisexual. I'm a lesbian.

That felt utterly liberating. Freedom, like I dropped 1,000 pounds of weight off my shoulders.

Olivia was incredibly supportive, congratulating me on embracing my true, authentic self, and reminding me that the timing didn't matter. "The timing of reckoning with yourself is perfect because it's happening now," she said. Her words were more than just encouragement—they gave me the reassurance and confidence I needed to face the world.

It was time to tell Connor once and for all—and sooner rather than later. Purposefully, I chose to write him a letter. Some might call it a cop-out, but for me, it was the only way. I've always been better with the written word, able to carefully articulate my thoughts, rather than stumble through an awkward conversation. Speaking off the cuff has never suited me. Writing gives me coherent thoughts I can't find in face-to-face conversations. Here's what I wrote:

Dear Connor,

Where do I even begin? We've been together for eight years—12 unforgettable years if you include our time dating. In that span, we've built a life, shared countless memories, and brought a beautiful daughter into this world. Through all the highs and lows, there's one thing that's never changed: our friendship.

You've been an incredible partner—always positive, always supportive, always dedicated. From the moment we met in Manchester Hall, me standing there in PJs, I was drawn to your charisma, your humor, and your unique spirit. You taught me how to find joy, even when life felt overwhelming. You showed me optimism when I couldn't see anything to smile about. And through it all, you stood by me with unwavering commitment, even when walking away would have been easier.

But now, it's time for me to be fully honest with you because you deserve nothing less. I've carried a secret for decades, fighting every demon to keep it buried. But I can't do it anymore. I can't keep pretending to be someone I'm not. Connor, I'm not straight. And I'm not bisexual. I'm a lesbian.

I've been hiding this truth since I was a teen—perhaps even younger than that, and I can't run from it anymore. I can't keep living like this. I need to live my authentic truth—for myself, for Quinn, and for the sake of my own survival.

Continuing in a polyamorous relationship no longer makes me happy. I want—no, I need—to explore my sexuality on my own, to date women exclusively. That's why I'm asking for a divorce.

Please understand that these past 12 years haven't been for nothing. I've spent an incredible part of my life with someone I can truly say is my best friend.

I'll always hold on to our greatest memories—like our first date, when you held me tight on Ride Jane's Carousel, and then watched Finding Nemo at the drive-in. Or the time we went to the Coldplay concert, singing "Warning Sign" at the top of our lungs. And of course, our unforgettable anniversary weekend in Vermont, hopping from vineyard to vineyard, distillery to distillery.

I know this will be difficult to process, and I'm here for you. When you're ready to talk or ask questions, let me know. I don't expect you to fully understand or be supportive right away, but I hope, in time, you'll find it in your heart to accept me for who I truly am.

I love you, and I always will.

Love,
Reilly

Howie barks, jarring me out of my deeply-rooted memory.

Oh, how Connor was shattered—devastated and angry, for what felt like an eternity. The months between our separation and divorce were heavy with tension and awkwardness, but somehow, we managed to navigate co-parenting Quinn without too much damage. Once the divorce was finalized, my relationship with Olivia faded, unraveling naturally as we drifted apart. Sometimes, I catch myself wondering what she's up to now. Is she still a unicorn, floating between couples? Or has she found her own version of a "happily ever after" with someone else? Looking back, I now realize that Olivia was a pivotal part of my journey in this lifetime. She was there to help me unlock my truth, showing me that everything unfolds exactly as it's meant to. I'll always carry deep gratitude for her.

As I guide Howie into the lobby of our apartment, shaking off the dusting of snowflakes, I can't help but think that even though it's painful to revisit the harder chapters of my life, there's value in reflecting on the journey. Reminiscing about Olivia always grounds me—reminding me of my awkward but inevitable entrance into the queer community, and how I was embraced with such grace and support. And that confession to Connor … what was once a symbol of despair and such overwhelming guilt now carries a completely different weight. It's no longer a reminder of what I lost but a testament to what I gained. It's the confession that set me free.

At home, I sink into the sofa, cradling a warm cup of tea and balancing my laptop on my knees. My mind feels clouded, drifting aimlessly. I was supposed to dive into the romance novel I'd promised myself, but instead, I find myself scrolling through work emails—103 unopened. And it's only 11:12 am. Is it too early for a cocktail? I wonder, half-joking. Maybe I can pretend I'm on vacation.

Hmm … hold on. That's not a bad idea. I should take a vacation. A solo vacation.

What better way to reconnect with myself on this year-long dating sabbatical. I can picture it now—pulling a Kate Winslet and Cameron Diaz in *The Holiday*, swapping homes with a stranger, retreating into some quiet, picturesque escape … and then, of course, meeting the love of my life. But, Reilly, I remind myself, that would totally go against our year of no dating. Five months in, single, and still loving it—no need to blow up things now.

I type "best vacations to take by yourself" into Google, while Howie curls up at my feet, his gentle breathing a steady rhythm in the background. Toronto pops up. Too close. Nope. Naples, Florida? Still feels too much like home. Nah. Costa Rica? Tropical storms this time of year. No, thank you.

I just finished watching a documentary last week called *Queer Japan*. That's it. Tokyo. Museums, gardens, historic temples. And I've heard the gay nightlife is incredible. I've always dreamed of exploring Japan's capital city—a bustling metropolis that never sleeps, filled with an electric energy that pulls you in.

Without a second thought, I check my calendar. Plenty of vacation days left to use before the end of the year. As long as I plan it for a week when Quinn is with Connor, everything falls into place. Scanning ahead, the first week of December looks perfect.

I'm not usually one for impulsive decisions, but this feels different— like it's meant to be. Flights booked. Hotel secured. I'll ask Alexis if she can watch Howie.

Tokyo, here I come.

CHAPTER **7**
pomegranate martinis

It's been one of those endless Thursdays. My off-site meeting at the Knickerbocker Hotel in Times Square has left my brain completely fried, the kind of mental exhaustion where even simple decisions feel like an Olympic event. Before heading back home, I take a long stroll down to Central Park, and Shake Shack's neon sign catches my eye. A Chocolate Salted Caramel Shake? Why not. It's the little things. What I really want, though, is a shot of whiskey chased by an ice-cold beer, but it's only 4:00 pm. A little too early to justify that indulgence … *for now*.

I find an empty park bench and sink into it, taking a moment to enjoy the surprisingly warm November air. Just a few weeks ago, we were buried under a foot of snow, and now, with Thanksgiving just around the corner, I'm sitting outside in nothing but a light jacket.

"Reilly—Reilly—hey, Reilly!"

Shit. All I wanted was a little peace and quiet. Who the hell is calling my name? I glance over my shoulder and spot Alexis jogging toward me. Great. The last time we really spent any time together was at her mom's funeral. Since then, we've only traded a few texts, and she dropped by once, about a month ago, to grab her favorite hoodie she left at my place.

"Hey, what brings you out this way?" I ask, trying to sound casual, feeling an odd blend of mild annoyance and a bit of excitement tugging at me.

"I was in the neighborhood for a SoulCycle class," Alexis replies, slightly out of breath. "Saw you from across the street and thought I'd say hi."

Despite just finishing a workout, Alexis looks as effortlessly gorgeous as ever. Her thick black hair is pulled back into a French braid, and of course, her makeup is flawless. Meanwhile, I'm here, slurping down this milkshake and feeling like a total fat ass in comparison.

I ask Alexis if she needs to get back to work, hoping to cut the conversation short. Truthfully, I'm not feeling particularly social today, and this was my polite attempt at a graceful exit. But Alexis, as usual, casually brushes it off, mentioning she's done for the day. Perks of being her own boss as a full-time content creator, she says—she decides when the day starts and ends.

Alexis hates the term influencer, but honestly, I don't see the difference. Brands pay her to promote their products—mostly fashion and beauty. She's got a solid following on Instagram and TikTok, and she's even launching her own podcast soon.

"Are you up for a drink?" Alexis asks.

In my mind, I'm already in PJs, eager to settle in for a quiet night. But if there's one thing I haven't quite mastered yet, it's saying "no."

We head over to The Aviary NYC and claim a small table tucked in the corner, surrounded by the hum of the early evening crowd. Around us, patrons are murmuring over their drinks, laughter spilling across the room in waves. Glasses clink in rhythmic bursts from the bar, a sound blending with the soft jazz playing overhead. The waitress hands us two drink menus, and as I casually scan the Fine Cocktails section, I catch Alexis sneaking a glance at me from the corner of my eye, her gaze lingering just a bit too long in the warm, dim light.

"I'm really glad we've reconnected," Alexis says evenly.

I force a half-smile, unsure how to respond. If I'm honest, I don't know how I feel about reconnecting. A part of me wonders what's really going on here. Before I can dig too deep into that thought, the waitress returns. I order a pomegranate martini, while Alexis goes for a glass of Merlot.

"Thanks again for coming to my mom's funeral," Alexis continues, her voice softer now. "I needed a friend more than ever."

"Of course," I reply, keeping my tone as neutral as I can. "It's always good to have a familiar face during something so heavy. And I knew a lot about your mom's cancer journey when we were togeth—uh, I mean … friends … or whatever we were." I say it bluntly, feeling the awkwardness between us. Really, Reilly, did you have to go there?

Alexis gives me an uncomfortable stare, shifting in her seat. "So … what's new with you?" she asks, clearly eager to change the subject. I can sense the tension beneath her words like she's still holding onto some resentment about how things ended. And, to be fair, I did end things immaturely. Toward the end of our friends-with-benefits situationship, I made it clear I was catching stronger feelings—I wanted something more. But Alexis? She was perfectly content keeping things casual, no commitment.

I finish the last sip of my first martini and signal the waitress for another round. That familiar buzz I crave is beginning to settle in, allowing me to relax and loosen up.

"I just booked a solo trip to Tokyo," I announce with a proud smile, feeling a spark of excitement. "I leave in two weeks."

Alexis's face lights up. "That's amazing! I'm so proud of you. That's so unlike you," she says, genuine surprise in her voice. "What are you planning to do while you're there?"

"Well, Quinn's got this obsession with skyscrapers, so I'm definitely heading to the top of the Tokyo Skytree. And I can't miss Shibuya Crossing—just to say I've been to the world's busiest intersection. I'll probably explore a few gardens, too, for some quiet time." I laugh, shaking my head. "You know how I usually have every second of a trip mapped out in advance? Not this time. I'm trying to embrace a new, more relaxed version of Reilly. I'm going to let my trip take me where it wants to go."

"Speaking of trips," Alexis says, a mischievous grin spreading across her face, "Remember that impromptu weekend in Catskills State Park? We stayed in that tiny, cozy cabin, and you spent four hours—*four hours*—trying to get the fire started." She bursts out laughing at the memory.

"How could I forget?" I chuckle. "I can't believe I didn't set my hair on fire trying to get that thing going."

Not that it really mattered. The fire wasn't the main event—we had one thing on our minds: sex. So we improvised, lighting candles and scattering them around the campsite. That weekend was one of the hottest. One of my favorites with Alexis.

I didn't expect us to start digging up old memories. Trying to steer the conversation in a different direction, I ask, "So, how's the podcast coming along?"

I genuinely want to know. But I also need to push away certain feelings that are creeping back in. "It's going great," Alexis replies, her eyes lighting up with energy. "I've lined up a producer from California to handle all the technical stuff—sound quality, editing, things like that. And my co-host and I have been rehearsing for weeks now, so I feel ready to go."

"That's awesome. I'm really happy for you, Alexis. It's amazing to see you getting this off the ground," I say, and I truly mean it. Watching her thrive in her career is exciting, especially since she wasn't always this driven.

"My work has been kicking my ass, as usual," I add, my tone shifting somberly. "I'm determined to make a career change someday, but I just haven't had the time to focus on it."

Alexis looks at me thoughtfully, then asks, "What is it that fuels your soul?"

She's always had a knack for diving deep, for steering the conversation into the places most people avoid. And that's just it—no one else makes me think the way she does. Maybe other people just don't want to go that deep, but with Alexis, there's no staying on the surface.

"I want to write," I say, the words spilling out without hesitation. "I want to pour my thoughts onto the page, to tell stories that are magical, memorable, and, most of all, mind-bending. I've always been shy and always struggled to express myself out loud. Somehow, I've managed to build a career in a job that I dislike—and, honestly, it dislikes me right back. But when I write? It's like something unlocks inside me. My thoughts become clearer, my creativity flows, and my heart opens in ways I can't explain. I want to share that part of myself with the world."

Alexis stares at me with that familiar intensity, the kind I've always loved. "Then why don't you do what's obvious?" she asks.

I blink, caught off guard. "What's that?"

"Quit your job and start writing."

The waitress drops off my third martini, and as I take a slow sip, I feel the warmth of the liquid on my lips. My mind starts to drift, the conversation with Alexis fading into the background as my thoughts begin to transport me somewhere else entirely …

The school bell rings sharply, cutting through the chatter, and the familiar shuffle of backpacks fills the room. "Don't forget, class—tonight is Parent Open House!" Mr. Langston's voice rises over the noise as his seventh graders pour into the hallway. "I look forward to seeing you all tonight!" he calls out, his smile visible even as we scramble toward our next class.

It's 7:15 pm now—a crisp fall evening. I'm walking through my junior high school with my parents for Parent Open House. The six-minute drive to the school was quiet, with NSYNC and Britney Spears playing softly on the radio. I begged them not to play the oldies for once.

Tonight, I feel different—there's an energy I don't usually experience. It's a rare sensation, and I know exactly why: my sister, Raegan, stayed home with a babysitter, and I've got my parents' full attention. Leading them through the cafeteria, the gym, and the library, I move with mild disinterest, my mind elsewhere. I'm saving all my excitement for one place— Mr. Langston's Creative Writing class. My favorite class of the day.

Once inside Mr. Langston's classroom, I proudly show my parents the books we've been reading. At my desk, I pull out a stack of writing samples from the school year so far. My parents' faces light up as they flip through the pages—A, A+, A++, A. The praise scrawled in red ink feels like a collection of small victories, each one validating my love for writing.

As we head out, Mr. Langston stands by the door, greeting and bidding farewell to everyone who passes through. He stops to shake my parents' hands, offering a polite goodbye. Then, with a firm, almost serious look, he glances at me, his expression shifting ever so slightly.

"Reilly, please dedicate your first novel to me when you become an author," he says, his tone more of a command than a suggestion.

His words have never left me. They're a quiet reminder of the belief he had in me—even when I wasn't sure I had it in myself.

Alexis snaps me out of my daze.

"Sorry, I got lost in an old memory," I say, shaking off the thought. "Oh, by the way, could you watch Howie for me while I'm in Tokyo?"

"Sure," Alexis replies without hesitation.

"Great, thanks a lot," I respond, relieved to have one less thing to worry about.

"How about I stay at your apartment while you're gone? That way, Howie can stay in his own space, plus your apartment is perfect for some new content creation," she suggests, her voice light but purposeful.

I pause, my fingers brushing the edge of my keys in my pocket. The thought of someone else inhabiting my space for a whole week makes my chest tighten with an unexpected reluctance. But … it would probably be better for Howie. And maybe it's not a big deal.

"Yeah, sure," I say, offering a small smile, trying to push aside the nagging hesitation. "That works."

"Oh! I just remembered—I'm going to be super swamped with podcast stuff and photo shoots over the next two weeks," Alexis says, her voice picking up speed. "Would it be alright if I came back with you tonight? You could show me everything with Howie—his routine, instructions, all that good stuff?"

Something about this feels a little off like there might be an ulterior motive buried beneath her casual tone. I notice Alexis's knee brushing against mine; it's been inching closer since the start of the evening. I know exactly where she wants this to go. And even though every part of me knows it's a colossal mistake, I'm not stopping it. "Sure," I say, keeping my voice easy. "I'll grab the spare key for you, too."

Her eyes lock onto mine, a slow, seductive gaze she's perfected. It's probably the alcohol talking, but there's something dangerously intoxicating about her. I can feel myself melting, helpless against the pull she has on me. It took me months to get over her, to piece myself back together after everything. Sleeping with her tonight ... will it unravel all of that hard-won progress? Technically, it doesn't really break any rules, does it? I'm not dating her, I reason, trying to ease the guilt building inside me. This is more like the break-up sex we never had.

The Uber ride back to my apartment feels thick with heat, like slipping into the old rhythm we once knew so well. It's almost unsettling how effortlessly our chemistry reignites—how natural it feels. Alexis leans over, her lips brushing my neck as she whispers filthy things in my ear, her breath warm against my skin. Every nerve ending flares to life, anticipation building like an electric current under my skin, sparking for what's to come.

Inside the elevator, Alexis pushes me firmly against the mirrored walls, her body melding into mine with a force that makes my breath hitch. The door dings open on the third floor, and we're met by the wide-eyed stares of the Eastmans—the elderly couple from down the hall. Their expressions shift from surprise to horror as we step out of the elevator and awkwardly switch places. At my door, my fingers fumble with the keys, my heart pounding as I try to unlock the door as fast as humanly possible. Alexis bites her lip, knowing exactly what that does to me, sending a jolt of heat straight through me.

We barely make it through the door before our hands are all over each other. Standing next to the sofa, I yank her jacket off, the fabric slipping from her shoulders. With a quick motion, I lift her tank top over her head, and she's already working to strip off my clothes, her fingers grazing my skin with every move.

We tumble onto the sofa, the urgency between us tempered by the soft give of the cushions. Our mouths crash together in a long, breathless kiss, our bodies alive with tension, charged with desire. The room fades away, leaving only the feel of her skin against mine, the pull between us growing with every touch.

I reach up and gently pull her braid free from the scrunchie, letting her thick, silky hair cascade over me, each strand brushing against my skin like a soft veil. My hands move down her body, gliding along her curves as we kiss with a hunger that seems to grow fiercer with every breath.

Her loud moans filling the air. I can feel her need rising, and as my fingers move in rhythm, her every sound drives my own desire to new heights, pulling me deeper into the moment.

I slide my fingers inside her as I trail soft kisses down her body. When my mouth finds her, I focus on her reaction, letting my movements become slow and deliberate, each touch measured and intentional. Alexis's back arches, her hands gripping the couch cushions as her body responds in pleasure, her release powerful and unmistakable.

As I kiss my way back up, Alexis wraps her legs around my waist, pulling me closer. It's my turn now, and she doesn't hold back. I sink into the couch, my breath already shallow as her mouth finds me with practiced ease, each movement precise. It doesn't take long before I'm overtaken by a flood of sensations, my body trembling as pure bliss washes over me. My climax, a breathtaking crescendo to an unexpected night.

And just like that, everything abruptly ends. The intensity dissolves into the quiet hum of the room, leaving only the sound of our unsteady breathing. Alexis pulls away, her expression shifting from raw need to something distant—just like it was in the past. Without a word, she swings her legs off the couch and starts gathering her clothes, the familiar routine of dressing filling the space between us.

I sit up, watching as she moves quickly, slipping back into her workout clothes and pulling her hair into a messy pony. There's a strange finality in the way she throws on her jacket like she's already halfway out the door. No lingering touch, no playful teasing, no conversation—just silence as she finishes getting ready.

"You know what?" I say slowly, carefully choosing my words as my frustration bubbles beneath the surface. "I think I'll just ask Connor and Quinn to take care of Howie while I'm gone. I wouldn't want to burden you with the responsibility—you've got so much on your plate already."

Alexis pauses, her eyes locking onto mine with an intensity that makes my chest constrict. For a brief second, I see the hurt flash in her gaze, but she quickly masks it with a cold indifference. "Well, if that's what you want—fine. I hope you have a nice trip," she adds, her voice clipped and brittle, each word landing like a sharp jab. Without waiting for a response, she turns and heads for the door, the silence between us suddenly feeling heavy and irreversible.

Standing there with one sock on and one sock off, I'm completely baffled by how quickly the night switched. What started as a casual run-in somehow spiraled into a chaotic mess of lingering tension from our past, sudden passion, and words left unspoken.

Whatever this was, I'm blaming it on the pomegranate martinis.

C**HAPTER** **8**
the flight

"**T**his is the final boarding call for Flight 806 with service to Tokyo," a voice chirps over the intercom, too cheerful for my liking. The flight number—seriously, is that an omen?

Thank God the airport bar is right next to the gate. I drain the last of my second Long Island iced tea, the ice clinking against the glass, and grab my carry-on with one hand, slightly unsteady on my feet as I rush toward the agent scanning the boarding passes.

I always wait until the very last second to board my flights. The less time I spend trapped in that metal tube hurtling through the sky, the better. I hate flying—more than hate, actually. It's more like a gnawing, irrational fear the moment I step foot in an airport. That's why I lean on Long Island iced teas and old Valium pills I've saved over the years. They're a delicate cocktail of superficial bravery, hopefully enough to get me through this 14-hour redeye flight to Tokyo.

Once aboard, I settle into my seat in Row F, Seat B—the middle seat, of course. The heavy buzz from my pre-boarding ritual is letting its presence be known. Pathetically, I'm already craving another drink, and we aren't even wheels up yet.

I reach into my backpack and pull out the book I picked up in the airport bookstore—*Journey of Souls: Case Studies Between Death and Life* by Dr. Michael Newton. An intense read to kick off a solo vacation halfway around the world, but my ever-growing fascination with past lives, the afterlife, and reincarnation leaves me deeply curious about the purpose of our lives.

I flick on the overhead light, and the sudden burst of brightness causes my seatmates to flinch. "Whoops, sorry," I mumble, offering a sheepish smile as they blink, adjusting to the glare.

About a half an hour into the flight, I spot the flight attendants rolling out the refreshment carts, and relief sweeps over me. Thank God—I need to keep this buzz going. Eleven dollars for a rum and Diet Coke? Completely absurd. But I shrug it off, reminding myself that I'm on vacation, and that's justification enough. I hand over my credit card without hesitation and even ask the flight attendant to swing by again in 30 minutes for a refill. Might as well make the most of this overpriced indulgence.

Two painfully slow hours go by. Sweaty and lightheaded, I feel a lump start to rise in my throat, tightening enough to make swallowing difficult. My hands start to tremble, my heart thudding steadily in my chest. With each passing second, an unease builds, creeping through me like a cold shadow. Fuck—I'm having a panic attack.

I try to steady myself, to keep calm, to blend in. My fingers grip the armrests as I fixate on the tray table latch in front of me, willing it to ground me, to stop the rising tide of panic. But my eyes won't stop darting back and forth, searching for something to anchor me. My breathing grows shallow as I fumble for the Gatorade in my backpack, unscrewing the cap with shaky hands. I take a few desperate sips, gulping down the liquid, praying it'll somehow pull me back from the edge.

Paranoia takes over, creeping in until I can't tell what's real anymore. Connor, Quinn, and Anna are suddenly sitting a few rows ahead, their mouths moving as they call my name, but their voices sound muffled, like they're underwater. I blink, and Alexis is here—as one of the flight attendants now, making her way down the aisle with another drink in hand, her eyes locked on mine.

Raegan, my sister, appears beside me, tears streaming down her face as she clutches a scrap of paper, begging me to watch her write her name over and over again. My heart races, and I can't focus. Everything around me feels too close and too far at the same time, distorted, as if I'm caught in a nightmare I can't wake up from.

The same visuals repeat on an endless loop, every time I glance up from the tray table. My mind feels trapped, stuck in a cycle. I gulp more Gatorade, my breath quickening, sweat dripping down my face. What's real and what's not? Am I dying? Is this what flashes through your mind on your deathbed? Did the plane crash, and now I'm crossing into heaven? My thoughts spiral further, spinning out of control. I'm losing it.

For the next hour, I fight an invisible war in my brain, gripping the armrests as if they're the only thing keeping me tethered to reality. Every muscle in my body is tense, straining not to slip back into the hallucinatory loop. I force myself to watch my phone timer count up to five minutes—again and again—desperate to cling to some sense of present life.

Finally, as the panic attack begins to subside, I'm left with a wave of exhaustion—and a crushing sense of shame.

My stomach churns violently, the unmistakable urge to vomit rising fast. Ignoring the seatbelt sign, I lurch out of my seat, practically climbing over my seatmate in a rush to the back of the plane. I barely make it to the bathroom in time, locking the door behind me before emptying everything I've consumed today. I spend the next 15 minutes hunched over the toilet, retching until there's nothing left.

When I return to my seat, dazed and weak, I can't shake the fear that I reek of sweat and vomit. My skin prickles with discomfort, and I try to shrink into my seat as if that'll somehow erase what just happened. What a miserable way to kick off this trip. But as I sit here, the weight of it all sinks in. This is the wake-up call I've been avoiding for years. I've been battling alcohol abuse for over a decade, but today … today is rock bottom.

Drained from the scariness of the last few hours, I grab the flimsy airplane pillow and threadbare blanket, sinking into my seat with a heavy sigh. I close my eyes, hoping for even a brief escape. But instead of rest, I feel myself slipping back into a memory I've stored away for years—one that surges forward now, as vivid and sharp as if it happened yesterday …

The slam of the pantry door downstairs jolts me awake, my eyes snapping open. My heart pounds in the stillness of my room, but I try to focus on the soft glow of the neon green stick-on stars on my ceiling, hoping their gentle light might lull me back to sleep. Maybe if I close my eyes tight enough, everything will be fine when I wake up. But through my slightly cracked bedroom door, I hear muffled voices—angry, tense. Dishes clatter violently in the sink, and the blaring music only makes it all sound more chaotic, more frightening. It sounds bad down there. Really bad. I need to check on Mommy and Daddy—make sure they're okay.

I slip quietly out of bed, my feet moving almost on instinct as I tiptoe toward Raegan's room. The hallway feels longer in the dark, every creak in the floorboards setting me on edge. When I reach her door, I pause. Raegan wouldn't understand what's happening downstairs. She's in her own world, a place where upheaval and commotion don't reach, where things stay simple. Her mind, with its innocence, perceives life in a way that feels untouched by complexity. She wouldn't grasp the fear building inside me, and explaining it would only make it worse—for both of us.

I peek through the crack in her door, reassured by the soft glow of her nightlight. She's safe in here. Maybe I should just go back to bed, and pretend it's all fine. But something in me says it isn't. Not tonight.

The yelling downstairs grows louder, sharper. Suddenly, I hear the back door slam shut, the sound vibrating through the house. My heart skips. Moments later, faintly through the havoc, I hear Mommy outside, banging desperately on the glass patio door, her voice rising as she begs to be let back inside. The helplessness in her voice sends a chill down my spine. I freeze, fear rooting me to the spot. What's happening?

Quiet as a pin drop, I creep my way halfway down the stairs, each step carefully placed to avoid the loud creaks. My heart races in my chest as I peek around the banister into the kitchen. There's Daddy, standing by the sink, rinsing dishes and pouring himself a glass of wine like everything's normal. But I see him stumble a little, unsteady on his feet, while Mommy's frantic banging echoes from the patio door. Her muffled pleas keep coming, but he doesn't even glance her way. My heart pounds harder. Why is Mommy outside? Why won't Daddy let her in?

I shout over the blaring music, my voice trembling. "Daddy, let Mommy back inside!"

Daddy whips around, his face flushed with anger. "Reilly, what are you—go back upstairs now!" His words are intense, cutting through the noise, making my stomach twist with fear.

But I don't back down. "Not until you let Mommy back in the house," I yell, my voice shaky, the weight of his fury pressing down on me. I know there'll be consequences—there always are—but I can't just leave her out there. Not like this.

With an exasperated sigh, Daddy marches to the back door and yanks it open, letting Mommy stumble inside. She's furious, her face flushed, eyes brimming with tears.

"You're a fucking asshole!" Mommy screams, her words slow and slurred, each one landing with venom. "How dare you lock me out!"

Her speech is thick, her steps unsteady as she wavers near the kitchen counter. But Daddy's no better—just as wobbly, his eyes glassy with the same intoxicated haze. The air between them crackles with unresolved anger, their bodies swaying under the weight of too much alcohol and too many words left unsaid.

"I never should've married you," she spits, her voice thick with emotion, barely holding herself upright. "You're a pathetic excuse for a husband." Her words cut deep, slurred, and laced with years of resentment.

Anxiety coils tightly in my chest as I rush down the stairs, my feet moving faster than I can think. I dart to Mommy's side, grabbing her arm, *my heart pounding. "Please stop yelling at Daddy," I plead, my voice small but desperate, my words tripping over themselves as I try to make sense of it all. I don't fully understand what's happening, but I know one thing—I just want it to stop.*

Daddy's eyes narrow, his expression darkening. "You won't even remember this tomorrow," he growls at her, his voice low and bitter. "Get a hold of yourself, Lisa."

"Reilly, why are you awake? Get upstairs now!" Mommy snaps at me, her irritation spilling over.

"I'm scared," I whisper, my voice trembling, barely audible over the turmoil.

"Go!" Mommy yells, her words sharp, wobbling as she stumbles toward the family room. But before she can make it, her foot slips on the step, and she crashes to the floor with a sickening thud.

"That's it," Daddy hisses through gritted teeth, his face contorted with anger. "Reilly, help me now."

"But Daddy, is Mommy okay?" I ask, my voice cracking, tears streaming down my face as I look between them, panic tightening in my chest.

"Just help me, now!" Daddy roars, his voice booming through the house, making me flinch. "Grab those bottles on the counter."

I hurry, my eyes darting over the scattered "adult drinks." Afraid I might drop it, my hands shake as I grab a bottle—unsure of what's happening but too scared to question it. I go back and forth bringing the bottles to Daddy one by one, who's waiting in the dining room. He's opened the bottom cabinet of the China hutch and is shoving the bottles inside. His movements are quick and deliberate like he's done this before. The whole time, my heart races, my mind spinning with questions I don't know how to ask.

He closes the cabinet with a sharp click, his figure looming over me. His eyes, glassy with alcohol and frustration, lock onto mine. "Don't tell your mother where I hid the alcohol," he says, his voice low and commanding, sending a shiver down my spine. His words hang heavy in the air, an unspoken threat.

Turbulence jolts me back to the present, snapping me out of that painful memory like a rubber band pulled too tight. My heart pounds as I blink back to the remnants of that night. That was my first ever encounter with alcohol—a bitter lesson at the age of eight. Watching your parent hide booze from the other, caught in a silent game of secrets and shame.

And that night was only the beginning. The first of countless negative experiences with my Boomer parents and their so-called "normalized" drinking. Every night after work, a glass of wine waited for them like clockwork, and it didn't stop until the *Late Show with Jay Leno* signed off. Weekends? The party started well before 5 pm. Wine glasses became just another part of the furniture, like the lamps on the side tables. It was all so routine—and so toxic.

Despite the routine, every morning my parents woke up, put on happy smiles, and played the roles of successful, generous, loving parents—functional alcoholics. But behind closed doors, alcohol was our family's dark secret—a constant source of disorder, heartache, and emotional instability. It caused parentification, escapism, and hypervigilance—the list could go on.

And now, I'm starting to see the same cracks forming in my own life. Quinn's already beginning to notice the difference between "sober Mom" and "drinking Mom," just like I did at her age. History repeats itself, and I'm following the same destructive pattern, passing down the very thing I swore I wouldn't.

As I sit here on this plane, awash in shame and guilt, I realize this has to be my turning point. The weight of my family's past is too heavy to carry any longer, and if I don't face my drinking problem head-on, it'll pass to Quinn—just like it did to me. I need to break free from the legacy of alcohol addiction before it tightens its grip on another generation. It's time to break the cycle, once and for all.

I take a deep breath, the first real one since I boarded this flight, and make a promise to myself: I'm going sober—cold turkey—from this moment forward. No more excuses. No more justifications. What better time to turn the page than on a once-in-a-lifetime trip as part of my year of self-discovery? Here's to fresh beginnings.

A small swell of pride rises in my chest as I sink back into the uncomfortable airplane pillow, the weight of my decision finally settling in. Next stop: Tokyo … as a teetotaler.

Chapter 9
coincidence

The scent of bamboo fills the air, subtle yet distinct, mingling with the soft, rhythmic sound of a waterfall just out of sight. I stand still in the midst of the Tonogayato Garden, letting the birds' lively chorus envelop me. The serenity here is almost intoxicating—a perfect contrast to the frenetic energy of NYC I've known for so long. No incessant car honking, constant sirens, and street peddlers … just serene beauty, calming energy, and mystical vibes.

It's my second full day in Japan, and I've finally shaken off the haze of my nightmare flight experience that brought me here. Today, I feel steady, grounded even, dressed in my signature look: worn-in jeans, a flannel shirt, a trucker hat, and my well-traveled white Adidas sneakers. Sure, I look like a tourist, with my backpack, camera, and guidebook poking out of my back pocket, but for once, I don't mind.

I find a park bench nestled among the greenery and sink into it, letting the stillness seep into my bones. Overhead, a Japanese bush warbler swoops past, its call slicing through the quiet as it vanishes into the canopy. I close my eyes for a moment, breathing in the scent of damp earth and pine, letting myself settle into the perfect solitude of this place. Six months into my year-long journey, my newfound easygoing approach to life, my vow to go sober—maybe this is progress, right? At least I'm not thinking about Alexis. That's good … isn't it? But then again … by reminding myself I'm not thinking about her, I'm still thinking about her. Ugh. I rise from the bench and continue along the garden's winding path, letting the quiet beauty guide me forward.

In a rare moment of spontaneity, I push past my usual shyness and approach a lesbian couple from Germany, asking if they can snap a photo of me on the rocky ledge, the majestic waterfall cascading behind me. The cool mist from the falls kisses my skin as I hand them my phone, and I can't help but marvel at how far I've come. Six months ago, the idea of approaching strangers would have sent me spiraling into self-consciousness. Now, I'm standing here, asking strangers to take my photo like it's no big deal.

As they frame the shot, I catch myself wondering: is their gaydar pinging right now? Are they picking up on my own subtle signals, or am I still that good at playing it straight? I glance down at my outfit, wondering if my demeanor gives anything away. The thought makes me laugh to myself, considering where my coming out journey started. Some days, I feel like I should just tattoo the rainbow flag on my forehead, I think, with a smirk.

As I meander along the shaded forest trails, I unexpectedly stumble upon a traditional Japanese tea house, its wooden structure blending seamlessly into the surrounding greenery. Drawn in by the peaceful aura, I step inside, pausing to slip off my shoes at the entrance. The smooth, cool wooden floor greets my feet, grounding me with a sense of quiet reverence. I settle cross-legged at one of the low tables, the air filled with the subtle scent of matcha and fresh tatami. The atmosphere wraps around me—calm, intimate, like a sanctuary hidden from the world.

When my matcha latte arrives, I cradle the cup in both hands, savoring the warmth before taking a sip. The earthy bitterness spreads across my palate, each taste note pulling me deeper into the moment as if nature itself flows through the tea. I pull out my travel book, its pages offering a map of endless adventure. I flip through, losing myself in the possibilities of tomorrow's exploration, the world outside this tranquil space feeling both distant and brimming with promise.

As the tea house begins to fill, the serene quiet gradually gives way to the soft hum of conversation, voices mingling with the faint clinking of cups. The shift in atmosphere gently nudges me, signaling it's time to move on. I pack my things into my backpack. Just as I prepare to stand, two women slide into the table seats across from me, their arrival halting my exit for just a moment.

"Hi, there. Nice to see you again," says one of the women in a familiar German accent.

It's the same lesbian couple from the waterfall. "Oh, hey." I respond, a little surprised. "Thanks again for taking my picture earlier." I assume our interaction will end there with a polite smile—after all, their English might be limited.

"Are you leaving?" the same woman asks.

Shit. So they can speak English well. Which means I should probably be polite and engage. Come on, Reilly. Step out of your comfort zone and make casual conversation—it won't kill you.

"Yes, I was just about to head out, but I actually—shoot—my God, I just realized I haven't gotten my credit card back yet," I reply, feeling a rush of gratitude that this chance encounter kept me from leaving without it.

"Oh, gosh. I'm glad you realized now and not later," says the first woman. "I'm Hannah, by the way." She gestures to the woman beside her. "And this is my wife, Mia. We're from Frankfurt, Germany. Where in the States are you from?"

"I'm from New York City," I say, offering a smile. "I'm Reilly."

"Ah, New York City!" Hannah's eyes light up. "That's on our bucket list. Are you traveling alone?"

"Yes," I say, feeling a bit more confident now. "I took a solo trip to do some once-in-a-lifetime sightseeing—but mostly to do some soul searching." I glance at my travel book. "I've got five full days left. Tomorrow, I'm heading to the top of the Tokyo Skytree."

"That's fantastic! It takes real bravery to travel across the world alone," Mia adds warmly.

"We went to the top of the Skytree yesterday," Hannah says. "The view is stunning, absolutely worth it. We still have a few days left ourselves—tomorrow, we're off to explore Tsukiji Outer Market."

I find myself genuinely enjoying the back-and-forth, so much so that for a moment, I forget all about my credit card again. The women spot the waiter, and flag him down for me.

"Well, it was lovely meeting you both," I say as I put my card back in my wallet. "Enjoy the rest of your trip!"

"You too! Já ne!" they say in unison, smiling.

"Já ne," I echo back, feeling a quiet sense of pride. I actually did it—made small talk with strangers I'll never see again. That's a big deal for me.

Back at my hotel, I step into the shower, letting the hot water wash away the fatigue from a full day of tourist activities. Each drop of water feels like a reset, leaving me refreshed and ready for the night ahead. Tonight, I'm venturing into Tokyo's gay scene—but, staying sober.

Standing in front of the mirror, I study my reflection, searching for the vibe I'm feeling. Confident or shy? Bold or cautious? The familiar temptation of alcohol hovers at the edges of my mind, whispering that it would smooth out the nerves, and make everything easier. But I push it aside. This is my chance to prove to myself that I can do life without alcohol, that I don't need the crutch.

Dressed in jeans, a crisp white t-shirt, and a black vest, I feel a sense of calm determination. As a final touch, I grab my trucker hat, flipping it backward. I chuckle at my reflection—there it is, the universal lesbian uniform, right? A silent nod to the community I'm slowly learning to embrace on my own terms.

My taxi weaves through the vibrant, neon-lit streets of Tokyo, the glow of signs reflecting off the windows as we approach Shinjuku Ni-chome, the city's LGBTQIA+-friendly district. Bars and clubs line the narrow alleys, each one beckoning with its own promise of adventure.

The energy of the neighborhood pulses around me as I step out onto the sidewalk, the air thick with energy.

I pull out my phone, quickly Googling the top must-see spots, feeling the familiar thrill of exploration. It wouldn't feel right to visit Tokyo without stopping by a sake bar, and just a block away is Eagle Tokyo—a cozy, low-key spot with a laid-back vibe. Perfect.

Inside, the space is intimate, the soft glow of dim lights casting a warm, inviting atmosphere. Prints of anime characters line the walls, their vibrant colors standing out against the sleek décor, while the steady pulse of Japanese techno music vibrates through the air, syncing with the rhythm of the night. I slide onto a barstool, feeling the nervous energy slowly fade, replaced by a sense of belonging.

I order a virgin mojito, the cool mint and lime, offering a refreshing mocktail. As I wait, my eyes drift to the TV overhead, where an unexpected scene plays out—American football, of all things. It's an odd yet comforting clash of worlds. Here I am, in the heart of Tokyo's gay district, sipping a mojito while watching a familiar slice of home flash across the screen.

Suddenly, I feel a tap on my shoulder.

"Reilly?" a voice exclaims, bright with surprise.

"Oh my God! Hannah, Mia!" I exclaim.

"I never thought we'd run into you again!" Hannah continues, her smile infectious.

"I know! What a coincidence. Are you sure you're not following me?" I tease. Yep, that confirms it. I'm feeling confident tonight—a welcome change from my usual self. I'm growing.

Hannah and Mia share a laugh as they turn toward the bar, their connection palpable. I watch as Hannah boldly steps up to order, her voice smooth as she requests a Tarazake for herself and a Daiginjo-shu for Mia. There's an effortless ease in how she takes the lead, exuding an assuredness that draws attention without trying.

Both of them are strikingly attractive, their chapstick femme aesthetic blending seamlessly—Hannah's sleek, understated style perfectly complements Mia's softer, more playful look. Together, they create a kind of symmetry, a natural balance that feels magnetic. And the energy between them? It's electric. It hums in the space around them, unspoken yet undeniable, like they're in sync on a level that doesn't need words.

"I think the universe is trying to tell us something," Hannah says, glancing over at a small table near the back of the bar. "How about we all hang out together? Join us?"

"This is the third time we've bumped into each other today," I laugh. "If that's not a sign from the universe, I don't know what is. Sure, why not?"

For the next two hours, we gab on and on—our travel itineraries, careers (which I reluctantly dive into), coming-out stories, and ex-girlfriends. The conversation flows effortlessly, each new topic spilling into the next like we've known each other for years. And so do the drinks—non-alcoholic for me—the energy of the night is intoxicating enough.

To my surprise, I've felt cool, calm, and collected the entire time. It's a stark contrast to the anxious mess I'd usually be in a situation like this, especially without my perceived "safety net" that's always been alcohol. But here I am—fully present, laughing easily, and enjoying the company of these two alluring women. It feels like I've found my rhythm, a new unlocked version of myself that's unburdened, more bold. Maybe, just maybe, I'm breaking my shell.

Hannah gets up to use the restroom, and as she passes behind me, her fingers lightly graze my shoulders and trail down my back. The touch is subtle but unmistakable, sending a flicker of awareness through me. Friendly … maybe a little too friendly. I can't help but wonder if it was intentional, a playful tease, or just an accidental brush.

Moments later, she returns, her eyes bright with mischief and a playful grin spreading across her face. "You know what we should do?" she suggests, leaning in just enough to draw me closer. "Dance and snap some embarrassing selfies—something to commemorate this random, totally unexpected meeting in Japan."

Suddenly, the calm confidence I've been savoring all night slips away. My stomach tightens, and a familiar wave of shyness crashes over me with brutal force. The idea of dancing—especially sober—sends my mind into a whirlwind of panic. My feet feel glued to the floor, my body locking in place as if trying to protect myself from whatever this moment holds. But before I can protest, before I can even form a coherent excuse, Hannah and Mia grab my hands, pulling me up with a burst of energy. And just like that, a rush of painful memories flood back, sharp and vivid …

Daft Punk's electric beats pulse through the packed Pure Nightclub in Las Vegas, each note reverberating off the walls. My little black dress clings to my body, its sleek fabric foreign against my skin, as I fidget with the bachelorette sash draped awkwardly across my chest. The room vibrates with energy, yet I feel completely out of sync—heels pinching my feet, professional makeup masking my usual face, French-manicured nails that don't quite belong to these hands.

None of this feels like me.

I steal a glance at the women around me—glamorous and poised, they belong in this glittering world of champagne and designer labels. Meanwhile, I can't shake the feeling that I'm clearly in the wrong life. My scene is a dive bar, playing darts, sinking into a booth with burgers and a cold beer, where the only soundtrack is laughter and the clink of glasses— not standing here in a swanky club, pretending to be someone I'm not.

These beautiful women sway effortlessly on the nightclub's tiered platforms, their bodies moving in perfect rhythm with the music. The flashing lights catch on their glowing skin, and the air buzzes with an ease I can't seem to tap into. You're at your bachelorette party, Reilly. You marry Connor in one month. The thought lands like a stone in my chest, heavy and suffocating. I force myself to smile, to push "happy" thoughts into my head, but they don't take root.

I will not let my eyes wander and linger on the women around me. Now is not the time to let myself feel any attraction toward women. Just one more month until the wedding. You can do this.

My bridesmaids surround me, their laughter and carefree spirits filling the space, while I awkwardly sip my drink, feeling disconnected from it all. I'm here, but I'm not here. Then, the DJ switches the track—Rock Your Body by Justin Timberlake—and suddenly, the whole room erupts with excitement. The familiar beat pulses through the club, and my friends' cheers rise above the noise, their voices echoing in the vast space like it's the anthem of the night.

Taylor, my maid-of-honor, grabs my hand and pulls me toward one of the elevated platforms. "Come on, Reilly! Let's do this!" she shouts over the music, her face lit up with pure joy. Her excitement is contagious, but I can't fully let myself feel it. I follow her onto the platform, my body moving almost mechanically.

My other girls join and dance without a care, singing along to every lyric as if the night couldn't be more perfect. But even as I force myself to move to the beat, the disconnect gnaws at me. I should be swept up in this moment, sharing in the ability to let go, but instead, I feel like a spectator in my own life—watching from the outside, pretending that I belong.

I stand frozen, every nerve buzzing with discomfort as if the spotlight has found me and all judgmental eyes are on me. Taylor reaches out again, her voice light, unaware of the storm inside me. "Loosen up, Reilly!" she laughs, dancing in front of me, her movements effortless, free.

I force my body to mimic hers, a half-hearted attempt to sway to the music, but it feels wrong like I'm moving through water. The panic surges through me, fast and unrelenting, making it impossible to stay. "I can't do this," I shout over the noise, my voice strangled with anxiety.

Before anyone can respond, I bolt down the steps, away from the blinding lights and the pressure. My heart pounds as I push through the crowd, leaving my friends behind in the swirl of music and laughter that I can't bear to be a part of.

The rest of my bachelorette party is spent sitting in a booth, nursing several drinks, and watching from the shadows. The weight of my own shyness presses down, holding me hostage in this invisible cage. Why am I always so stuck—so afraid? Why am I so trapped in my own body—in more ways than one?

"Woohoo, let's dance!" Hannah exclaims. Somehow, Hannah and Mia manage to get me to the dance floor. The bar hums with the vibrant pulse of Japanese house music, and for a fleeting moment, I let myself get swept up in the energy, my body moving tentatively to the beat. For just a second, it almost feels natural—almost.

But then, a familiar twinge of anxiousness creeps in, unraveling the confidence I've borrowed from the room. My mind starts spinning, and suddenly I feel too exposed, too seen. Maybe holding a drink will help, I think as if the simple act of gripping a glass could shield me from the weight of my own insecurities.

I slip away from the dance floor, weaving through the crowd until I reach the bar. I order another virgin mojito, the energizing beverage I hope to calm my nerves.

As I wait for my drink, the steady pulse of the music fades into the background, replaced by the noise in my head. My mind begins to drift, slipping away from the present moment again. The bartender places the mojito in front of me, but I barely notice it as another memory surges to the surface—unbidden and vivid, as if it had been waiting for the right moment to strike …

It's Senior Breakfast, just two days before high school graduation, and I'm sitting with my pod of closest friends. We're laughing, joking, enjoying what feels like one of the last carefree moments before life changes for all of us. Ms. Baker, our beloved senior class teacher, stands at the front of the room, calling out awards—superlatives voted on by our peers. The atmosphere is light and playful.

"And the next superlative category is Shyest Girl and Shyest Boy," Ms. Baker announces in an exaggerated, meek voice, making the room chuckle. There's a sinking feeling in the pit of my stomach. My name better not be

called. Don't worry, Reilly, it won't happen. No way. I'm graduating with 850 students. No one even knows who I am.

Ms. Baker's voice cuts through the anticipation of the room. "And the Shyest Girl goes to … Reilly Trenton!" Her words echo in my ears, but everything else fades. I don't hear the Shyest Boy's name. All I can focus on is the sudden rush of blood in my ears as my peers laugh at us for winning this ridiculously stupid award. The spotlight shines on me as I make my way to the stage, feeling exposed.

"1,000 yen … mojito," the bartender says, snapping me out of that painful memory from my high school days. I pay the bartender before heading back to Hannah and Mia. As I approach them on the dance floor, I realize I've left my phone at our table, and the thought strikes me—I really want to get some pictures of us dancing. I tell them I'll be right over.

But as I head back to the table, one last painful memory floats to the surface, uninvited and sharp …

It's a crisp fall day in the early 1990s—Bring Your Child to Work Day. I'm seven years old, my small hand clutching tightly to the soft, white fabric of Mommy's pharmacist coat as we make our way through the hospital corridors. The sterile scent of disinfectant lingers in the air, and the gentle buzz of activity surrounds us.

Suddenly, a loud, piercing noise shrieks over the intercom, startling me. My heart jumps, I have no idea what code blue means. My eyes dart around, expecting franticness, but everyone seems unfazed, continuing with their work as if the commotion were just part of the routine. I grip Mommy's coat even tighter, feeling both small and out of place in this grown-up world.

Mommy leads me around the pharmacy department, her hand resting gently on my shoulder as she points out the towering shelves of medications, each bottle and box neatly lined up like building blocks. We pass the compounding rooms, where faint chemical smells persist, and I catch glimpses of other pharmacists in their white coats, working with precision behind glass windows. The workstations hum with quiet efficiency, computers clicking and printers whirring softly.

Throughout the day, Mommy introduces me to her co-workers one by one—the same repeated words over and over again. "This is Reilly, my terribly shy child," she says with a smile each time, her words both familiar and stinging. "My other daughter, Raegan, is the talkative one." And then she laughs like clockwork.

I shrink a little more with each introduction, the label of shy settling over me like an invisible weight. I just smile politely, feeling diminished.

Snapping back to the present, this cold memory remains like an old scar freshly reopened. Throughout my childhood, the words "terribly shy" cut deep each time they were spoken, it felt like a branding mark pressed against my skin. I grew up carrying that label, believing that shyness was something bad, something to be ashamed of, rather than simply a part of who I was. It wasn't just a descriptor; it became an identity, one I tried desperately to shake but couldn't escape. And the weight of it has followed me into adulthood, always hanging around in the background, whispering that I am less than, that something about me isn't good enough.

Back with Hannah and Mia, my non-alcoholic mojito in one hand and my phone in the other, I snap a few selfies of the three of us, their smiles contagious as we huddle together for a shot. The bar's lively energy buzzes around us, and for once, I don't feel the usual urge to pull back. Our night is just beginning, though I have no idea just how much more it will unfold.

My anxiety, which had been hovering at a low vibration all evening, quietly begins to fade. I can't help but wonder—could this be a breakthrough moment? Perhaps rehashing these memories was the medicine I needed to gain a new perspective.

It feels like the memories I unlocked tonight needed to be set free—reopened and exposed—like I'm finally unburdening myself of a character trait that's unnecessarily held me back for far too long. For the first time, I'm beginning to live more openly, without the weight of my shyness pressing down on me. That shyness has shadowed me my entire life, fueling my anxiety, low self-esteem, and the fear of being truly seen. Not anymore.

Maybe meeting Hannah and Mia was no coincidence—more like a spark, helping me shed this skin I've worn for 34 years. It feels like I'm on the verge of something new, something lighter. There's a certain energy around them like they've appeared in my life at the perfect moment.

The beat pulses through the bar, and the entire vibe has shifted into something electric, alive. The dance floor has filled up since we claimed our spot in the center, and for the first time ever, I feel completely uninhibited. The usual weight of self-consciousness is gone, replaced by a sense of liberation that feels foreign.

Hannah and Mia have been dancing together all night, their bodies inching closer and closer toward me, their movements fluid and effortless. Are they flirting with me? I can't quite tell, but at this moment, it doesn't matter. I'm caught up in the rhythm, lost in the music and the warmth of the space between us. I dance with Hannah, then Mia, and before I know it, I'm sandwiched in between them, the three of us connected by an unspoken dynamism that pumps through the air.

Hannah leans in close, her body brushing against mine, the scent of her shampoo drifting over me. The proximity sends a shiver through me, and suddenly the air between us shifts, charged with anticipation as if the room itself is waiting for something to happen.

"We think you're incredibly sexy, Reilly," Hannah whispers, her voice low and enticing. Her eyes meet mine with a smoldering look. "What if we made our trips even more memorable? Join us back at our hotel after this."

Stunned is an understatement. My pulse quickens, and the heat between us intensifies. I turn fully to face Hannah, locking eyes with her as a seductive smirk tugs at my lips. Fueled by confidence, inhibition, and maybe a touch of recklessness, I murmur, "You got it, babe."

We waste no time once we're inside their hotel suite. The room smells faintly of weed and cappuccinos, a curious combination that somehow suits the evening. Hannah and Mia are quick to close the space between us, their lips meeting mine, pulling me into them. Am I really doing this? My thoughts swirl for a brief moment, but I shake them off—after all, this will make one hell of a story. Hooking up with two beautiful women, total strangers, after a night of dancing and laughter in Tokyo—it's something that could only happen on a trip like this.

The glow of Tokyo's skyline spills softly into the room, casting shadows on the king-sized bed. Music hums in the background, setting the mood. Hannah's lips find mine, and I respond eagerly, losing myself in the present. Mia moves behind me, her hands slowly peeling away my clothes. My fingers graze up under Hannah's sweater, and as I touch her warm skin, I feel the electricity between us escalate. She kisses me along my neck, soft and deliberate, tugging at my shirt to reveal my collarbone. The heat rises between us, a crescendo that pulls us deeper into this moment together.

Turning around, half-undressed, I catch Mia's gaze and pull her in close, kissing her deeply, letting everything else fade away. My hands slide down to her waist, gripping her firmly before slipping beneath the fabric of her pants, feeling the softness of her skin. There's something magnetic between us, a kind of pull that I can't quite describe. Hannah watches from the bed, her body bathed in the soft light shining in from the window, waiting for us to join her.

We strip away the last of our clothing and crawl over to Hannah, our bodies fitting together naturally like we've done this a thousand times before. Mia's lips find mine again while Hannah gently kisses my back, her mouth tracing soft lines down my spine, sending shivers through me. With a slow, deliberate touch, she parts my legs, her warm breath grazing my skin as her kisses move lower.

Pleasure ripples through me as Hannah explores my body with her tongue, each movement thoughtful, teasing. Mia's hands wander over my chest, caressing my breasts before she moves above me, straddling my face. Her scent envelops me as I respond eagerly, my tongue matching the rhythm of her body moving on my mouth as she holds onto the bed's backboard for balance.

The room is filled with the sound of our shared pleasure, our moans blending together in a symphony of sensation. It feels like time has slipped away, and all that remains is this moment, this connection between us.

I shift my attention to Hannah, her lean, fit body stretched out beneath me. Her eyes meet mine with a quiet intensity as I gently press her back into the mattress. I take my time, teasing her with soft kisses and gentle flicks of my tongue, savoring the sound of her quiet gasps as I explore her. Behind me, Mia's hands and lips add another layer of thrill, and I'm lost in the euphoria of it all—giving, receiving, completely immersed.

We all collapse together in a tangle of limbs, breathless and alive. There's a kind of peace that settles over us as we exchange a slow, lingering kiss—each of us savoring the warmth and closeness we've found here, on this unexpected night.

As the evening carries on, I realize this trip to Tokyo will forever be etched in my mind, not just for the adventure, but for the way it's cracked me open, allowing me to finally step out of my shell and into a version of myself I've been too afraid to embrace.

CHAPTER **10**

the holiday party

It's been a week and a half since I returned from Tokyo, and I have to admit—my self-esteem has never felt higher. I'll never see Hannah and Mia again, but the incredible serendipity of our meeting prolongs like a cherished treasure, a fleeting connection that feels almost too perfect to belong to this world. It's the kind of experience that binds itself to your soul, reminding you that, once again, the universe gives you exactly what you need—and when you least expect it.

The stapler jams for the fifth time as I try, unsuccessfully, to staple the agency's 20th copy of the year-end report. Seriously? I mutter under my breath. Why is it that the simplest tasks always turn into the most frustrating ones?

I glance at the clock—already 10 minutes late for the fourth quarter recap meeting happening in the agency's lobby. Perfect. I slip into the back just as the CEO launches into a self-congratulatory spiel about J/PR's phenomenal metrics this year. Around the room, there's a collective exhale—phenomenal metrics mean end-of-year bonuses, after all. With that, everyone's already mentally checked out, their thoughts drifting to the holiday party waiting for us on the 30th floor.

At the party, I make my way through the crowd, sipping on a virgin margarita. I'm only half disappointed that it's not the real thing. Honestly, it feels good to wake up with energy these days—but nights like tonight, filled with awkward small talk among colleagues, makes the craving for alcohol buzz around my mind like an annoying mosquito.

Suddenly, the sound of clinking glass pierces through the chatter. The room quiets as our VP Director of Strategic Initiatives takes center stage, raising his glass high. "As we raise our glasses tonight, my fine people, I want to take a moment to reflect on the hell of a year we've had. This year started out shaky but, as always, you guys are warriors— you conquer the impossible …"

My God, he makes us sound like we're out there fighting combat missions. This is public relations and marketing, for Christ's sake. This exaggerated rhetoric is one of the many reasons why I can't stand what I do anymore. With the toast over, I reluctantly return to the forced conversation that awaits me among my co-workers. I try steering the topic toward business, but as always, it takes an inevitable nosedive into workplace gossip.

"I can't believe Kendall is here with that two-faced, narcissistic boyfriend … I thought she dumped him last month," Andrea relays.

"Ever since Brett got that promotion, his ego's tripled in size," Caitlin sounds off.

"I'm still shocked Jordan lost that new business pitch. She shouldn't be allowed to touch sales again until she proves herself," Mark chimes in.

Ugh, this aspect of corporate life drains me. The endless rambling, the same empty conversations—I'm over it. I can only fake interest for so long before I need a way out.

In my mind, Alexis's voice echoes from that night we had our post-breakup rebound sex: "What is it that fuels your soul?" I know one thing for certain—it's not public relations. It's not this endless mingling with superficial colleagues at swanky holiday parties, pretending to enjoy the company of people who by day are nothing more than corporate monsters, hungry to make a quick buck off brainwashed businesses.

What I want is to work from the sanctuary of my own home. Peace. Quiet. No more phoniness and corporate nonsense. No more schmoozing clients and kissing up to CEOs. I want to write. I want to tell stories that pulse with passion, authenticity, and love. I want my words to crystallize into something real, something that transports readers to places they've never dreamed of, challenging their minds in ways they've never considered. That's who I'm meant to be.

I sigh, realizing I'm probably years away from realizing this dream—if it ever happens at all. Another virgin margarita is calling my name, so I make my way back to the open bar. The jazz band softly plays *Chestnuts Roasting on an Open Fire*, the melody mixing with the sounds of laughter and light conversation.

The bartender hands me my virgin margarita, flashing a wink as he says, "I think it's really cool you're sober."

"Thanks," I reply, though my voice lacks the enthusiasm to match the compliment.

"You're cute," he says, leaning in just a little closer. "Can I take you out for coffee sometime?"

I'm completely caught off guard. It takes me a moment to find my words. "Oh, um, I'm gay. But thanks for the offer."

As I scurry away toward the sanctuary of the charcuterie table, I can't help but think, that was weird. How did he not know? I'm the only woman here not wearing a cocktail dress. Maybe I still come off way more straight than I realize.

Just before I reach the food, Linda, our VP of Marketing, and Megan, the Director of New Business, stop me in my tracks with their husbands by their sides.

"Reilly, one second. I want to introduce you. This is my husband, Ryan," Linda says exuberantly as I reach out to shake his hand.

"And meet my husband, Adam," Megan adds proudly, beaming as I offer a polite nod and the obligatory nice-to-meet-you smile.

"Hi, I'm Reilly. It's great to meet you both," I say, my voice carrying my new confidence. "I'm the Director of PR."

Linda, with all the ignorance of small talk, casually asks, "Is your husband meeting us here soon?"

In an instant, my mind transports me to a memory with Olivia, unearthing itself from deep within …

The windshield wipers move furiously as the rain pours down in sheets, making it hard to see anything in the pitch black of a late November night. As we round the corner of the gravel road, the warm glow of WhistleWood Farm Bed and Breakfast comes into view, its windows lit up, beckoning us from the hill. I pull the car up front, grabbing our bags when Olivia surprises me on the driver's side, pulling me into a hard, passionate kiss— the kind of kiss you only see in the movies.

"I just wanted to kiss you in the rain," she whispers, her voice soft but intense, as we stand there getting completely drenched.

I grin, heart pounding, feeling the undeniable pull of desire. "Let's get inside and check in," I say, the excitement of the weekend with Olivia ever increasing—just the two of us, no Connor.

Inside, the crackle of a fireplace fills the cozy common area, and the tables in the dining room are already set for tomorrow morning's breakfast. The ambiance is perfect—warm, cozy, and brimming with charm. Although we have grand plans of hiking the trails and visiting a few wineries, I have a feeling we'll be spending most of our time in our room.

An older gentleman appears out of nowhere—likely the owner— offering us a welcoming smile.

"Checking in?" he asks, already knowing the answer.

"Yes, the reservation is under Berkeley. Two nights," I reply, my voice steady.

"Ah, yes. Right here." He proceeds to check us in, explains the details of the property, and informs us about breakfast timings.

Then, with a friendly nod, he says, "I hope you sisters have a great stay with us here at the WhistleWood Farm Bed and Breakfast. If there's anything I can assist you with during your stay, just let me know."

Sisters?

"Reilly, are you alright?" Linda asks, jolting me back to the present.

Everyone thinks I'm straight. The bartender. My colleagues. Even bed and breakfast owners who see me check in with another woman, for Christ's sake. After waiting 34 years to get to this point in my life, I'm ready to make it obvious to the world—I want to live openly as a queer woman. Or at least give off bigger signals that I identify with the LGBTQIA+ community.

The next morning, I'm up early—eager and alert, and, thankfully, hangover-free. Sitting in my hair stylist's chair, I mull over some bold ideas to change up my look. What if I go full rainbow? Maybe a mohawk? I turn to my stylist, feeling a surge of confidence, and say, "Shave it."

Two hours later, I sit at West 4 Tattoo, staring down at two potential designs. My nerves are buzzing—I'm about to permanently alter my body—but I'm ready to make a statement. It feels like the right kind of self-expression, something to cement the authentic me.

It's 5:00 pm—time to pick up Quinn at her friend's place. I catch my reflection in the mirror, admiring the decisions I've made today. It's funny how a couple of changes to my appearance can trigger this burst of confidence, making me feel more connected to the LGBTQIA+ community than ever before. An overwhelming urge to text Alexis bubbles up inside me. I know she shouldn't be the first person I want to share exciting news with—not after how things ended that one night— but I can't shake the feeling that she'd get it, that she'd appreciate this.

(5:09 pm) Reilly:
Hey, what are you up to?

(5:10 pm) Alexis:
Just chillin', watching Lifetime. 😁

(5:14 pm) Reilly:
Guess what I did today?

(5:15 pm) Alexis:

What?

(5:17 pm) Reilly:

I got an undercut and a Gay Pride tattoo! I'll send you pics.

(5:18 pm) Alexis:

OMG ‼️ Really?! I'm so proud of you.

(5:19 pm) Reilly:

Thank you!

(5:21 pm) Alexis:

Hey, are we okay after that night?

(5:23 pm) Reilly:

Yeah, we're okay. 😉

The evening flies by in a blur of laughter and lightness. Quinn and I order Chinese takeout and settle in to binge-watch *Love Island*. Once she's in bed, still riding the wave of confidence from today's choices, I retreat to my home office. Sitting at my desk, I glance down at my new tattoo on my wrist and smile. For the first time in years, I open a Word document on my computer and just let thoughts spill out, unfiltered and raw. Two hours pass in a blink. Exhausted but satisfied, I head upstairs to bed.

As I'm about to climb under the covers, my phone buzzes with a text from Alexis.

10:27 pm (Alexis):

And BTW, that undercut is fucking sexy.

CHAPTER 11
book club

*T*he gas pump clicks off with a thud, signaling the tank is full. I twist the gas cap back on my mom's brand new 2016 Mercedes G-Class, the icy air biting through my coat as I shiver against the chill. Settled back into the luxurious warmth of the heated passenger seat, I forget all about the frigid air outside.

Like a well-rehearsed speech, my mom sets the guilt trip in motion, the rhythm of this conversation is as predictable as an old song. "You know, Raegan misses you," Mom says evenly, the practiced tone of disappointment laced with her words. "You're her only sister, and she doesn't have much in her life. It wouldn't kill you to visit her more often. Or call her more frequently on the phone."

I feel the familiar pang of shame shoot through my body. "I know," I murmur, regret heavy in my voice. "I'm sorry. With work, Connor, and the baby, I have so much going on lately. But I know, I know—I shouldn't be making excuses." I pause, trying to temper the edge in my voice. "It's just that Quinn is everywhere now—she just learned how to walk—and your house, Mom … it's not exactly baby-proofed. I'm afraid she'll break something or hurt herself."

Mom scoffs, her disapproval lingers in the air, thick and unspoken. Then, she completely pivots with a smile that doesn't reach her eyes. "So … how's your job going?"

I let out a slow breath, grateful for the shift but all too aware of the unspoken judgement hovering beneath it. "Work is going well," I offer, forcing some brightness into my tone. "I actually got a raise last week."

Her face lights up, almost too quickly, as if flipping a switch. "Oh, that's wonderful, Reilly! I'm so proud of you!" she exclaims with enthusiasm. "I can't wait to tell your dad."

I nod, absorbing the praise like a sponge, but it never quite fills me. Instead, it leaves me feeling rather hollow, like I'm soaking up water that slips right through the cracks.

As a kid, my parents praised me often. They relished in my athleticism, my academic achievements, and my "good girl" model behavior. They felt proud of my upbringing, maybe even leaned into it with a kind of relief. That's because they never could give my disabled sister, Raegan, the same kind of life as me—and I always sensed my parents' guilt because of it.

Raegan was born prematurely four years after me with cerebral palsy and epilepsy, destined to live with physical and cognitive disabilities her entire life. The doctors didn't expect either her or my mother to survive the day she was born. But they did. Against all odds, they both made it through. And because of that, Raegan became a miracle child—proof that life, no matter how fragile, can defy expectations.

Growing up, I got to do it all—sports, sleepovers, school dances. I earned my driver's license, stayed out late with friends, and got to pick my college. And Raegan … well, she didn't get to do any of those things. Raegan's life moved at a different pace, one defined by limitations I never had to consider.

In a way, we were raised separately, though it wasn't by design. Back in the '80s and '90s, my parents coped with what life handed them by keeping our worlds apart. I think it made things easier for them. Raegan had her activities, and I had mine. Our lives rarely intersected—except when Raegan had a seizure or other medical issues. Or when I discovered the neighborhood kids mocking her. That's when my protective instincts kicked in, and suddenly, I was deeply involved in my sister's life.

The snow falls steadily as we turn onto Berkshire Street. Every year, Mom and I attend a holiday-themed wine tasting at a local winery near my childhood home. It's a tradition, though tonight, the icy roads make me wonder if we should have stayed in. Quinn, who just turned one, is back home with Papa and Raegan. I picture them—Quinn's boundless energy, Raegan's quiet, watchful presence—and turn my attention back to the road. The snowplows are working hard, trying to clear the way. We've got four more miles to go, all winding country roads until we reach the winery.

The familiar sounds of the Bruce Springsteen channel from SiriusXM radio fill the car, a kind of background hum. We've driven in silence for the last few miles, both lost in thought. The tension sits between us as it often does. I shift in my seat, the warmth of the heated leather pressing against my back, and awkwardly break the silence. "So … how many bottles of wine do you think we'll bring home tonight?"

"My guess is 10," Mom says with little hesitation. "You know, I've got to buy all those Christmas presents for my co-workers."

I smirk. "My guess is 20. 10 for you, 10 for me."

The road ahead is pitch black—no street lamps, just open farmland stretching into the void. The snow is falling harder now, the flakes thickening in the headlights' glow. I glance at the dashboard. 8:06 pm. The darkness feels oppressive, wrapping around the car like a heavy blanket. "Mom, you should turn on your brights," I suggest, my voice tighter than before.

"The selection of whites better be good this year," she chimes in. "I always end up with too many reds …"

Suddenly—

Blaring headlights explode out of the darkness, bearing down on us. "MOM! YOU'RE RUNNING THE STOP—"

SMASH.

Everything goes dark.

I snap back to the present, the memory hitting me like a punch to the gut. Today marks eight years since Mom's sudden death. The pain remains, raw and unyielding, hovering just below the surface, refusing to release its grip. Earlier, I called Dad and Raegan to check in; they sounded somber yet went about their routines, treating today as if it were just another day. But for me, it feels like an open wound that time hasn't healed.

Grounding myself, I take in the stunning penthouse apartment, where vaulted ceilings soar above, blending modern sleekness with rustic charm. Exposed wooden beams lend a cozy radiance to the contemporary design while floor-to-ceiling windows capture a breathtaking view of the NYC skyline—a glittering sea of jewels against the night sky. Casually dressed in boyfriend jeans and a royal blue button-down, I sink into the plush sofa, nestled between a hetero couple in their 30s and a sharp-eyed, feisty-looking middle-aged man named Barry. Around the room, others mill about, as the lively murmur of conversation begins to soften.

"Alright, everyone, let's find our seats," Eric, our book club leader, announces with a calm yet commanding presence. "Before we dive into the depths of this book, I'd love to hear your initial thoughts—just overall impressions."

I reach into my bag and pull out my well-worn copy of *Journey of Souls: Case Studies Between Death and Life* by Dr. Michael Newton. I first picked it up at the airport bookstore on my way to Tokyo, unaware of how deeply it would resonate with me. Since returning, I've devoured the book three more times, captivated by its profound exploration of past life regression hypnotherapy, reincarnation, and the afterlife. So when I stumbled across this local book club and saw *Journey of Souls* on the reading list, I signed up in a heartbeat. It felt like a sign—another one of those rare moments when everything falls into place.

Sitting here among these strangers, bound by the shared experience of reading this masterpiece, I feel a spark of excitement—a surge of passion to write my own work of art. The idea of one day being discussed, analyzed, and dissected in book clubs fills me with a sense of purpose, as if my voice, too, might someday resonate with others the way this book has with us.

Ashton, a kindergarten teacher in her early 40s, is the first to speak. She leans forward slightly, her voice steady and sure, her expression calm but resolute. "This book has given me the answer to the question we all ask: What happens after death? Life isn't a one-time experience. We live 100s of lives."

Jordan, a 35-year-old web designer sitting across from me, nods thoughtfully. "What's fascinating to me is that under hypnosis, all these case studies recount a very similar experience of what happens right after death. It's like … all people remember traveling the same path, taking the same journey to the spirit world."

Caitlyn, a college student at NYU, jumps in eagerly. "I love the idea that when we die, our soul meets our individualized spirit guide. And then, we're reunited with our spirit family. It's … comforting, you know? Like we're never truly alone."

I can feel the shift in the room as Barry, sitting beside me, crosses his arms and leans back with a smirk. He cuts in with a derisive snort. "I think it's a load of horse shit. When you're dead, you're dead. There's no such thing as past lives, soulmates, or reincarnation."

A tense silence follows Barry's words before Eric speaks, his voice measured and calm. "How do you know that, Barry? Do you have proof that those things don't exist?"

Barry doesn't miss a beat. "I don't need proof," he says with a casual shrug, unfazed. "It's just what I believe."

"Everyone is entitled to their own opinion and beliefs," Eric says evenly, his gaze lingering on Barry before shifting back to the group. "This book offers a glimpse into the afterlife for those curious about what lies beyond death, and in doing so, it opens Pandora's box to an array of profound questions: What is the process of reincarnation? How do our past lives shape our present lives? Can souls communicate with the living? What role do spirit guides play? Is it possible to access memories from our previous lives?"

His words hang in the air, and I feel a pang in my chest. This book hits harder for me than most here will ever realize. My mind drifts back to that horrible night eight years ago. Mom died on impact. With the snow falling and the roads slick, she ran a stop sign, and a pickup truck, barreling at 40 miles an hour, slammed into us. I walked away with a broken arm and a few cuts. But she was t-boned and died instantly.

The relief I feel now, knowing she felt no pain, is immeasurable. Newton's research gives me something even greater—a belief that her soul transitioned to the spirit realm, that her journey didn't end that night. Her soul lives on, and that knowledge has become my anchor, keeping me steady when the weight of her loss feels too much to bear.

And then diving deeper into the book, there's Newton's research on soulmates. Through past life regression hypnotherapy, his patients revealed that we travel from lifetime to lifetime with a group of souls—a soul family. Ten to 15 souls who are destined to impact our lives, teach us, and love us in each lifetime. It resonates with me deeply—it explains why certain people feel like home the moment I meet them, and why some connections run deeper than anything logic can explain.

Feeling a sudden rush of enthusiasm, I lean forward on the sofa, waiting for the right moment to jump in. As the conversation pauses for a beat, I can't hold back. "As a companion piece," I blurt out, my voice rising with eagerness, "we should read *Between Life and Death* by Delores Cannon." The words spill out faster than I intended, but I'm too caught up in the moment to care.

Eric smiles, nodding with approval. "That's an excellent idea, Reilly. It's a quick read, and we don't have anything planned for the next two weeks. Let's go for it." His easy acceptance sends a spark of validation through me, and I can't help but feel a small thrill at the thought of diving deeper into this exploration together.

After the book club wraps up for the night, I head home, the concept of soulmates still swirling in my mind. As I let my thoughts drift and process this enlightenment, it dawns on me that soulmates aren't just lovers—they're anyone who significantly brings impact and value to our lives, and leaves a lasting mark. These are the people who show up again and again, in each of our lifetimes, connected by something far greater than coincidence.

So, who are they—the souls bound to me through time? The ones destined to walk beside me, lifetime after lifetime, woven into the fabric of my existence no matter how many lives I've lived or how many more I will? Who are the spirits that rise and fall with me, always finding their way back, as if the universe itself insists we meet again?

Connor immediately comes to mind—I feel he is a constant companion who walks beside me through every life we share. What we have transcends connection; it's deeper. In this lifetime, we created Quinn. I feel it … in every lifetime, he's there, like an unbreakable thread woven through the fabric of our existence—a bond that, no matter where or when, endures as a profound friendship in its purest form.

I think a little harder, and Olivia surfaces. She may no longer be part of my present-day life, but her importance can't be understated. In this lifetime, she was the catalyst—the spark that set everything ablaze and forced me to confront my ultimate truth. In every lifetime, I imagine she finds me, and something about her—her presence, her actions—shifts the course of who I am.

I feel certain that Quinn is one of my soulmates—always a shining light in my life, a guiding force who lifts me even in the darkest moments. I envision each lifetime, she pushes me to become a better person, her presence a gentle reminder of who I am and who I'm meant to be. With her, there's an ease, a sense of familiarity that defies words, as though our souls recognize each other beyond the limits of this world.

And then there's Alexis. But questions linger, heavy and unresolved: Are we soulmates, or is she simply a trigger, someone placed in this life to teach me lessons I need to learn? Her presence is so intense, so all-consuming, that it blurs the lines. Could someone in my soul family make me feel this way? If she were truly part of that deeper connection, would our relationship always be this tumultuous, or is that friction the very lesson I'm meant to grasp?

CHAPTER 12
kinkster

The weekend arrives, and February's sharp, biting cold clings to me as I step into the warmth of an inviting bookshop on the corner of Waverly Place. The moment I cross the threshold, I'm enveloped in the familiar, comforting aroma—earthy paper mingled with the faint must of old books, the soft leather of well-worn couches, and the rich, homey scent of freshly brewed coffee swirling in the air. I breathe it all in, a quiet thrill settling in my chest as I anticipate a few hours of uninterrupted reading and escape. There's something about this place, like a reset button for my mind—a welcome change of scenery that seems to realign everything.

I lose myself almost immediately, completely absorbed in Delores Cannon's *Between Death and Life*. The words flow like a current, carrying me effortlessly deeper into the mysteries of reincarnation and the afterlife, each page drawing me further away from the world around me. It would take something loud—very loud—to pull me from this trance. And then, it happens—a nearby conversation, sharp and intrusive, cuts through the quiet like an unwelcome guest, tugging me away from my focus.

In the next aisle, two voices rise above the tranquil silence of the bookstore, their conversation distinct enough to break the spell of calm. Curiosity piqued, I peer through the gaps in the bookshelf. An attractive couple stands there, engrossed in their discussion—far too animated for a conversation that seems more suited for a private setting. Their body language is intimate, their words low but intense, as if the world around them has disappeared and they're in a bubble of their own.

"Daddy, did you get the notification from FetWorld?" the woman teases, her voice playful yet suggestive. She's dressed in a figure-hugging black dress, a bold statement necklace resting against her collarbone, catching the light. "We need to get our tickets for FetishCon if you still want to go," she adds, her tone dripping with anticipation as if the mere mention of it is a secret thrill they share.

"Yes, Babygirl," the man replies, his voice a perfect balance of authority and tease. Dressed sharply in navy trousers, a crisp white collared shirt, and loafers, he exudes control. "Did I give you permission to speak?" he asks, his tone soft but firm, the edges sharp enough to make the woman's playful smile falter. "You'll be getting a spanking when we get home, my princess," he adds, the promise hovering in the air like a looming mystery between them.

Daddy? Babygirl? Princess? My gaze stays with them a moment longer. They look like a married couple—similar in age, both wearing wedding rings, their polished appearance a stark contrast to the words slipping between them. Their playful, provocative exchange feels massively out of place here, among the quiet shelves and whispered pages of books. It's as if they've brought an entirely different world into this space, one that shouldn't belong but somehow demands attention.

And then, just like that, my mind drifts, untethered from the present, spiraling back in time … pulling me into a memory I hadn't expected to revisit … ever.

I'm sitting in a dimly lit, seedy sex club on Bourbon Street, one year ago. The air is thick with the stench of stale booze, sweaty bodies, and something else I can't quite place, but none of it really matters. Alexis appears from the bar, effortlessly balancing two oversized hurricanes, their neon-red contents threatening to slosh over the rims. I watch her, captivated by the sway in her hips as she navigates the crowd, her walk a perfect mix of confidence and seduction. She slides back to our rickety bar table, eyes gleaming with mischief. This weekend was her idea—an impromptu getaway to New Orleans to blow off steam. Or, as she likes to say, "to not take life so damn seriously."

"I can't believe we're about to watch a live sex show!" Alexis shouts over the thumping bass and the chaotic buzz of the crowd, her eyes wide with excitement. "I've seen and done a lot of things, but this … this is a first."

I laugh, the alcohol buzzing warmly through my veins. "I'm excited too! Or maybe I'm just really drunk," I slur, giggling as the words stumble out. "We've been drinking since, what, 10 o'clock this morning?" I add, swaying slightly, my laughter spilling out as easily as the neon-red liquid in our drinks.

"Ooh, here comes the first couple!" Alexis exclaims, leaning in closer as the lights dim and a hush sweeps over the crowd. The atmosphere shifts instantly, thickening with anticipation, the energy in the room almost palpable as everyone holds their breath, waiting for what's about to unfold.

Fake candles flicker, casting shadows that dance across the walls. A man and a woman emerge from a side door, their movements slow, deliberate, oozing a teasing sensuality. It's almost like a dance, their bodies winding around each other, drawing out the tension until, piece by piece, their clothes slip to the floor. What follows is a fever dream of thrusting, grinding, and riding—an intoxicating blur of bodies and heat. The crowd roars and whistles with every movement, their excitement building with each rhythm, the room pulsing with raw, unapologetic lust.

Every 10 minutes, a new couple takes the stage, seamlessly swapping out performers like clockwork. After five acts, the energy in the room shifts as a lesbian couple steps through the side door, instantly re-capturing the crowd's attention. The air feels charged, an almost electric curiosity rippling through the audience, as all eyes lock onto the stage.

"Reilly, look—it's girl-on-girl next," Alexis says, her voice tinged with fascination, her eyes glued to door the performers enter. She's completely mesmerized, but my mind is elsewhere, drifting. I glance at the worn mattress on stage, my thoughts snagging on how stained and grimy it looks. When was it last cleaned? Ever? The thought alone sends a shiver of disgust through me. Gross.

One of the women is clad in a black leather dominatrix outfit, the glint of a whip catching the dim light as she holds it with practiced authority. Her partner stands before her, blindfolded, wrists bound in handcuffs, a quiet vulnerability radiating from her posture—softness, and submission contrasting sharply with the other's poised control. The air between them feels charged, a silent tension that's as palpable as the leather and metal binding them.

"This is sexy, don't you think?" Alexis leans in, her breath warm against my ear, cutting through the noise and chaos of the club. Her voice is low, intimate. "I'd love to role-play with you … experiment with domination and submission." The suggestion endures, charged with the kind of thrill that only comes from breaking boundaries.

I sit there, still and pensive, my heart pounding in response. The idea of Alexis controlling me sexually sends a rush of heat through my body, igniting something raw and primal deep inside me. My thoughts race, spiraling as I struggle to maintain composure. She has no idea how much that suggestion turns me on—how badly I want to surrender to her, to feel that power shift between us.

"Yeah," I reply, my voice low, trying to keep it steady and cool. "I'd be down to try anything." The words hang in the air between us, charged with a discreet promise that sends a spark through the space. I shift closer to her, the sexual tension rising between us as I press a slow, deliberate kiss to her cheek.

Alexis turns to me, her eyes dark, locked onto mine with an intensity that steals my breath. "You will be my perfect kitten," she whispers, her voice thick with seduction, each word like a caress. A full-body shudder ripples through me, electrifying every nerve, and leaving me buzzing from *head to toe. The fire in her voice lingers, sparking an untamed desire deep within me.*

The steady jingle of patrons entering and leaving the bookshop pulls me back to the now. The kinky couple is gone, but the echoes of their conversation stay—a glimpse into the world of dominance and submission, where the lines between role-play and reality blur into the dynamics of a master and his Babygirl. It's intriguing, really. Alexis and I dabbled in this seductive play in our own way—a dominant femme and her submissive—but neither of us ever fully embraced the roles. Like so many things between us, it fizzled out, fading quietly into the background, as if it had never taken root at all.

Still nestled in my cozy chair, I drift into a daydream, envisioning the intoxicating thrill of surrendering to a powerful, domme femme. She'd carry an electric presence—commanding, self-assured, with an edge that sends a shiver down my spine. I can almost hear her voice, firm yet comforting, as she guides me, bossing me around in a way that's both thrilling and safe. I imagine her rewarding me when I'm good, delivering just punishment when I'm not, her dominance as sharp as it is nurturing. And in the midst of all that control, she'd cradle me in her care, holding me close, balancing authority with a tenderness that makes me feel like her cherished little princess.

I used to think only Alexis could embody that dominant femme persona I craved so deeply. But I see the truth—it was never just her. The thrill runs deeper than one person; it's the allure of any woman who carries herself with commanding confidence and control that sends tingles through my body. The thought of surrendering, both in bed and beyond, pulls me in, like a magnetic force I can't resist. It's the power dynamic itself—the intoxicating dance of authority and submission— that truly captivates me, filling me with an excitement that's as much emotional as it is physical.

I try to refocus on my book, but the thought of a kinky lifestyle clings to the edges of my mind, creeping in no matter how hard I push it away. And then I remember the app—FetWorld. What if I downloaded it? What if I made a profile? There's nothing wrong with a little harmless curiosity, right? The idea of exploring my fetish tugs at me, tempting me to really delve into that side of myself. After all, this is supposed to be my year of self-exploration. Maybe there's no better time than now to indulge a little. It's not dating, not really—so I wouldn't be breaking my own rules, would I?

My curiosity wins. With a hesitant breath, I pull out my iPhone and open the App Store. Slowly, almost cautiously, I type in "FetWorld," my fingers trembling just slightly. Sure enough, the app pops up—the same one that the couple was talking about earlier. Bold letters flash across the screen, the tagline daring me to dive in:

Love kink? Chat. Meet. Mesh. Unleash your kinky superpowers. Meet kinksters like you.

The words feel provocative, and electric, sparking something inside me that's hard to ignore. I take a deep breath, the weight of the moment settling over me like a heavy blanket. My finger hovers for just a second longer, knowing there's no going back from here. And then, with a quick tap, I hit download.

Here goes something.

CHAPTER 13
raegan

Signs of spring are finally breathing life back into the city. Flowers are erupting in bursts of color along the sidewalks, while tender green leaves are unfurling from every tree branch, stretching toward the warmth of the sun. New York City hums with renewed energy, a vibrant pulse that weaves through the streets, touching everything and everyone. The past nine months of my self-imposed dating hiatus—reside vividly within me, urging me to reflect on all that has shifted and grown within my soul.

Full disclosure—I've had a few distractions … but nothing that's crossed into real dating. There was that impulsive, after-work rendezvous with Alexis, the reckless yet thrilling threesome in Tokyo, and, of course, a current detour into the world of kink. Sigh. I mean, I'm only human, right? Surprisingly, each of these experiences has nudged me closer to my own growth, leading me to discover parts of myself I hadn't yet explored.

The smooth roadway beneath me threads through winding country roads toward New Paltz—veins running through the rolling hills outside the city—as I let my thoughts drift. I'm on my way to Dad's and Raegan's house to lend a hand. The steady hum of tires on asphalt creates a meditative rhythm, each passing mile syncing with the ebb and flow of my mind. This two-hour drive has always been my sanctuary—a quiet stretch where the noise of daily life fades away, making space for deeper questions to rise like echoes from within.

Who was I in past lives? What patterns have I broken, and which ones still cling to me like shadows? Am I growing, or am I still running in circles, avoiding the hard truths?

I arrive in New Paltz—the town that shaped my early years. It's as charming as ever, with its sprawling vineyards, white picket fences, and American flags fluttering in the breeze. Driving down the familiar streets, I pass the ice cream shop where I worked every summer during high school. So many memories are tucked within those four pastel-painted walls. I remember the awkwardness of pretending to have crushes on boys who'd drop by for a late-night cone, all while secretly harboring feelings for the girls. It's surreal, almost like stepping into a time capsule, to think about how far I've come since then.

As I wind through my neighborhood street, the houses stand like silent sentinels of my past, watching over the years I've left behind. I pull into the driveway of my childhood home, a place seemingly frozen in time. Almost everything looks as it did 20 years ago. A few cosmetic upgrades have been made, but the essence of it remains untouched. The tree where I carved my initials at eight years old still stands tall, its bark weathered yet proud, like an old friend who's kept my secrets. A bird's nest still sits snugly between the drainage pipe and the garage, the soft chirps a familiar melody that hasn't changed over the years. The navy blue shutters still frame the windows, perfectly matching the light blue paint of the house—a color scheme that has quietly withstood the test of time.

I turn off the car and take a deep breath, the weight of anticipation settling in my chest. Visiting Dad always feels like a gamble—it could be a joyous reunion, full of laughter and stories from the past, or it could be a triggering affair, where old wounds are quietly reopened, leaving me feeling remorseful and drained. As I sit in the stillness of the car, the uncertainty hangs heavy in the air, and I can't help but wonder—what if Mom was still alive?

Inside, the atmosphere sharply contrasts with the serene calm just outside. *Law & Order* reruns blare at full volume, the dialogue bouncing off the walls like a relentless drumbeat. The microwave has been beeping incessantly since the moment I walked in. Raegan's dog, Ninja, scratches frantically at the back door, his claws scraping the glass as he whines to be let in, adding to the symphony of chaos.

Papers are strewn haphazardly across Dad's kitchen table—medical records, Medicare paperwork, Social Security checks, and a jumble of other important documents. The clutter tells its own story, a silent testament to the constant battle of keeping everything in order. In the other room, Raegan is quietly absorbed in a puzzle, her favorite pastime, finding solace in the simplicity of pieces fitting together in ways that life rarely does. Meanwhile, Dad's voice echoes from the hallway, tinged with frustration as he tries to untangle a billing mess with his medical insurer—a problem that slipped through the cracks months ago. He's been on hold for over a half an hour, and the weariness in his tone mirrors the weight of responsibilities piling up around him.

I let Ninja in, stop the microwave's constant beeping, and turn down the TV to a reasonable volume. I breath deeply. The chaos subsides, and already the space feels a little calmer. Ever since Mom's sudden passing, I've noticed a slow, steady decline in Dad's emotional and physical health. The weight of being both a widower and the full-time caregiver to a disabled adult child has taken its toll on him, inch by inch. His once magnetic presence has diminished, replaced by a quiet exhaustion that clings to him like an invisible burden, growing heavier with each passing day.

That's why I'm here today—to help Dad get his and Raegan's affairs in order, just in case something unexpected happens. His memory isn't what it used to be, and proactivity goes a long way. When Dad can no longer care for Raegan, it will be me to step in. I need to know exactly what to do, to be prepared when that time comes, to ensure that Raegan's taken care of. This inevitable responsibility hovers like a shadow over everything, an unspoken weight that reminds me how quickly life can shift, and I need to be ready to carry it all.

"Okay, Dad. I brought two binders—one for your affairs and one for Raegan's. As we gather and organize everything, we'll keep the information neatly sorted in these," I say, my tone firm, letting confidence guide me as I step fully into this role. This is uncharted territory, but it's a role I know I need to shoulder.

"Reilly, I can't thank you enough for helping me get organized," Dad replies, his voice carrying a hint of worry. "I wouldn't even know where to start."

"I've got you, Dad," I say, my tone softening with reassurance. "We'll get through this together."

We start with Dad's binder. I jot down all his passwords, write a list of his doctors and their contact information, note his medications along with their dosages, and figure out which bills are on autopay and which still need to be paid manually. The list seems endless, each task a small piece of the bigger picture, but slowly, we begin to make sense of it all.

Then we switch to Raegan's binder, which requires much more detailed information about her daily routine and lifestyle. From a list of her caseworkers to the stores where we buy her adaptive equipment, everything is carefully recorded in this file keeper. Each detail is important, ensuring that when I step in next I know exactly how to maintain the rhythm of her life.

Phew! That was a lot to get through, but it was necessary. Now, with everything neatly tucked away in these two binders, relief settles over me. When the inevitable day comes, everything I need will be right here—organized, accessible, and ready.

It's 4:00 pm, and, like clockwork, Dad pours himself a glass of wine, offering me one as well—but I decline. Raegan wanders into the kitchen, munching on her favorite afternoon snack of pretzels and hummus. I try to strike up some small talk with her, but it feels like an uphill climb, like talking to a three-year-old. Her cognitive impairment makes conversation nearly impossible, and Dad, ever the vigilant protector, stays nearby, listening to our every word. He often jumps in, speaking for Raegan as if she can't voice her own thoughts.

It's frustrating—just once, I'd love to have a genuine, uninterrupted conversation with my sister, even if it's nothing profound.

As we trudge through choppy dialogue about Raegan's dog, Ninja, and what she's going to eat for dinner, my mind swirls back to the past, landing on a distant memory of one of our family vacations at Walt Disney World. I was 13; Raegan was 9 …

The stifling July heat presses down on us as we stand in line for It's a Small World—for the third time today. Raegan's face lights up, practically vibrating with excitement to ride her favorite attraction … again. I, on the other hand, am biding my time, my patience tested as I quietly wait for my chance to go on some thrill rides.

"Can we please go on Space Mountain or Splash Mountain next, Mom … Dad?" I chime in, my voice edged with nagging impatience at this point.

"Reilly, for the 50th time, your sister can't handle those rides, not with her seizures," Mom replies, her tone firm. "And I don't like the idea of you going by yourself. First, you're too young. And, second, this is a family vacation—we're supposed to stick together."

"How about we compromise and go on The Haunted Mansion after this?" Dad suggests, his tone enthusiastic, clearly trying to appease me.

I grumble under my breath. Everything is always about Raegan. My frustration builds with each passing minute—this is my vacation, too, dammit.

I beg one more time. "Please, pretty please, can we at least try Splash Mountain? It's only one drop at the end, and we'll get wet—it will feel so good in this heat!"

Mom and Dad exchange a weary glance, one of those silent conversations they've mastered over the years—no words needed. I've been nagging them for the past hour, and I can see the fatigue in their eyes. They just want me to stop.

"Alright … we'll do Splash Mountain after this," Mom finally says, her voice tinged with reluctance.

"Thank you! Thank you!" I exclaim, unable to hide my excitement. "Raegan will love it."

About 30 minutes later, we finally reach the front of the It's a Small World line. We wait a bit longer for an accessible boat, making it easier for Raegan to climb in. As we glide along the water, the cheerful music fills the air, and the whimsical animatronics sway and twirl before us. I watch Raegan light up with pure joy, her face glowing as she sings along to the familiar tune, her voice soft but filled with elation. She eagerly points out her favorite characters, her eyes wide with wonder as we pass each one by.

A pang of guilt tugs at me for being so whiny earlier about the rides I wanted to go on. Watching Raegan now—so happy, so completely in her element—makes me realize just how much these moments mean to her. And maybe, they mean more to me than I care to admit. Her joy is infectious, and as much as I wanted my own thrill, this—seeing her light up—feels like the real gift.

After the ride, we step back into the boiling heat, waiting as Dad studies the park map to figure out how to get to Splash Mountain. I can hardly contain my energy, already imagining how I'll brag to my friends at school about conquering the famous ride. Maybe it'll even boost my "cool factor" a notch or two.

But just as I'm getting swept up in my anticipation, I glance over at Raegan, and my heart stops. Something is wrong. Her face has gone pale, and her eyes are starting to roll back in her head.

"Mom, Raegan is having a seizure!" I scream, my voice cracking with panic.

In an instant, Mom drops her lemonade and lunges toward Raegan, catching her just before she collapses onto the unforgiving concrete. With a practiced but urgent motion, she gently lays Raegan down on the ground. My sister's body convulses violently, drool spilling from her mouth, and I notice with a sinking heart that she's wet her shorts. Then comes Raegan's scream—a piercing, gut-wrenching sound that slices through the air—the familiar shriek that's lodged itself deep in my memory, where it will remain etched and haunting for the rest of my life.

Dad reassures the concerned onlookers, his voice steady as he insists that our family has everything under control and there's no need to call the paramedics. Disney staff members approach us, their faces a mix of concern and professionalism, but once again, Dad calmly diffuses the situation. Despite his composure, I can feel the weight of all those eyes on us, staring, making me feel exposed and tense like we're some kind of spectacle.

About 30 minutes later, Raegan has fully come out of her seizure. She's talking again, her voice weak but stable. Mom and Dad turn to me, their expressions a mix of exhaustion and regret.

"Hey, kiddo. We're not going to be able to do any more rides. We need to get your sister back to the hotel to get cleaned up and to rest," Dad says bluntly—I can already sense the finality in his words.

The excitement I felt earlier has long since evaporated, replaced by a dull ache of disappointment. So much for riding Splash Mountain. And with this being our last day at Disney World, I know I won't get another chance. Tomorrow morning, we fly home, and the adventure I'd been so excited for ends with a sigh instead of a splash.

My mind pops back to the present, standing in Dad's kitchen as he pours himself his second glass of wine. I never did get to ride Splash Mountain. I heard they tore it down a couple of years ago and replaced it with something new. Just as much as I've come to realize the world gives you what you need in the right moment, it also serves as a reminder that life doesn't always give you what you want.

Being a sibling to someone with disabilities hasn't been easy. Growing up, there were no bike rides or rollerblading adventures to share. I couldn't confide in Raegan about boys—or, in my case, girls. When I got married, it struck me that I would never stand by her side at her wedding or be the aunt to any children of her own. And one day, I will take over as Raegan's primary caregiver simply because I'm her one and only sibling. It may sound harsh, but I didn't choose this life.

Or maybe … I did.

This realization strikes with clarity, like one of Raegan's puzzle pieces clicking into place. The idea that I might have selected this life—

selected Raegan as my sibling—settles over me with a strange sense of sharpness. In the quest for information about my evolving spiritual beliefs, I've learned this is how souls transition back to life on Earth. Maybe this was the universe's design all along, shaping me into someone capable of understanding the challenges others face—their limitations, their resilience, and what it means to move through the world with empathy. I just need to do a better job of living that understanding.

As I watch Raegan enjoying her snack, I see not just my sister, but a teacher—a guide in my soul's existence. She embodies a kind of pure love and innocence that reminds me how life's complexities can be a gift, a means to evolve in ways I never could have imagined. Through her, I glimpse the deeper purpose behind my own hardships—a calling to advocate for those who deserve equality, respect, and love. Perhaps this lifetime was always meant to be more than just an existence. Maybe it was a choice—a choice to grow into a more compassionate, understanding soul.

This moment feels like the start of something new between Raegan and me. I haven't always been the most patient, empathetic, or accepting person toward her. Perhaps this is a step toward healing—a chance at redemption. Acknowledging the distance that has stood between us, I wonder how things might have felt different if inclusion and acceptance had been valued as much then as it is today. But rather than dwelling on what might have been, I choose to focus on what I can do now—to bridge the gap between us and create a future built on empathy rather than regret.

As I gather my things to head back to the city, something pulls me back. Maybe it's the realization that every moment with Raegan is a chance to make up for lost time in the simplest of ways. I walk over to one of the cabinets of Dad's entertainment unit, and reach in for her favorite board game—a small gesture, but one that carries the weight of a deeper connection I'm ready to embrace.

"Raegan, you up for an intense game of CandyLand?" I ask, my voice joyful and enthusiastic.

Raegan's resounding "Yes!" warms my heart, reminding me that it's never too late to build the bond we missed out on growing up. Today, we're not just playing a game—we're rewriting our story, one colorful card at a time.

CHAPTER 14
mistress mackenzie

Hiding my phone beneath the boardroom table, I feel a rush of adolescent nostalgia, like I'm back in eighth grade, trying not to get caught passing notes in class. The glow from the screen casts a faint light on my lap, but I can't resist. Alexis and I are locked in a conversation that feels almost absurdly deep for a Monday morning. Generational trauma and the pathways to healing—it's the kind of discussion only we would be having while the rest of the world is still rubbing the sleep from its eyes.

A quiet chuckle escapes me, but I quickly stifle it. The last thing I need is for Mr. Portman, the president of J/PR, to catch me zoning out. The absurdity isn't lost on me—here I am, surrounded by talk of profit margins and market shares, while my thoughts are miles away, unraveling the complexities of inherited pain and the delicate art of moving beyond it.

I slip my phone beneath my leg, wedging it between the chair and my thigh, and force myself to reengage with the discussion at hand—performance metrics and industry trends for The North Face's latest business proposal. This PR pitch could be a major win for J/PR, potentially catapulting us to a new level. Everyone's on high alert, ready to contribute, but as Mr. Portman rambles on about outdoor apparel, I feel a deep craving, an aching for an escape from the corporate grind.

I'd give anything to be tucked away in a cozy coffee shop right now, rain tapping softly against the window, typing away at my laptop and breathing life into the novel I'm working on—*a woman who teeters on the edge of death, only to realize it wasn't her time to go. She returns with a newfound purpose, rising to become one of the most influential figures of her era, her legacy etched into the history books read by generations to come.* It's a story of second chances, of defying the odds to realize her potential. Maybe, in some ways, it mirrors my own journey—an unfolding narrative where the protagonist is still discovering the depths of what she's truly capable of.

A gentle vibration pulls my attention back to my phone. Alexis again, I assume. I swipe to reply, ready to tell her I'll catch up later. But as I unlock the screen, I notice the notification isn't from Alexis. It's a match alert from the FetWorld app. My stomach tightens as I read the bold, message: A KinkStar wants to talk to you! Beneath it, the name "Mistress MacKenzie" stares back at me, bold and commanding.

Mistress MacKenzie. The name rolls through my mind, sultry and intense, lingering like smoke from a smoldering flame. A slow smile tugs at my lips, unbidden. Now, that—I pause, savoring the thought— that sounds sexy.

I quickly realize that opening the app here in the office is a bad idea, so, with a hint of disappointment, I slip my phone back down underneath my legs. But deep within me, I'm smiling—my heart racing with a mixture of anticipation and butterflies. To my surprise, the workday zooms by—a full day of meetings, a client-catered lunch, and a relentless stream of emails. I do my best to stay focused, but Mistress MacKenzie shadows my thoughts, swirling like a thrilling, unshakable distraction. The thought of talking to a domme femme is intoxicating. I can hardly wait until I'm home.

Back at my apartment, after walking Howie, calling Quinn, and downing a protein smoothie for dinner, I finally collapse onto the sofa. It's a beautiful April evening; the sun sets, casting warm, golden rays through my floor-to-ceiling windows. The eagerness has been building all day, simmering just beneath the surface, and now, at last, I can finally open the message from Mistress MacKenzie. Watch, Reilly, I tell myself—it will probably end up being nothing. But as I tap the app, a jittery thrill bubbles up, refusing to be silenced, my fingers trembling slightly with expectancy. My breath catches as I read the message, the words unfurling with confidence.

(9:34 am) Mistress MacKenzie:

> Hi, Babygirl. I'm Mistress MacKenzie looking to find my sissy slave. You caught my attention with your puppy dog eyes and gorgeous smile. Message me back.

My heart pounds in my chest, a mix of intrigue, surprise, and curiosity. The directness, the power in her words—it's both exhilarating and terrifying. I stare at the screen for a moment, unsure of how to respond. Part of me wants to jump in and explore the thrill of submission, while another part hesitates, wondering what this might unlock inside me.

(7:13 pm) Reilly:

Hi, Mistress MacKenzie. Nice to meet you.

I press send, and anxiety floods in almost instantly. Why didn't I say more? I should've gotten into character and played the naughty slave right back. Ugh. I probably blew my chances of this going any further right there. Patiently waiting for a reply feels unbearable as I reread my message over and over. My thumb hovers over the screen, tempted to send a follow-up, but then my phone dings. My heart skips a beat, the sudden rush of adrenaline making my fingers tremble. She responds.

(7:18 pm) Mistress MacKenzie:

Hello, darling. I am so happy to hear from you. What brings you to the app?

Relief washes over me. My chest loosens, the weight of anticipation lifting just enough. Type back, Reilly. Don't overthink it. Just type. But as the excitement churns inside me, I can't help but pause. What do I even say? The words form slowly and deliberately, as I take a breath and begin typing.

(7:21 pm) Reilly:

I was curious about the D/s lifestyle and wanted to check it out.

(7:22 pm) Mistress MacKenzie:

Have you ever had a mistress before? I am an experienced domme to my submissives. 15 years. Tell me your kinks/fetishes and I'll make them come true.

Tingles shoot down my spine. My pussy begins to throb. Holy shit.

I click open Mistress MacKenzie's profile—44 years old, bisexual, living in Cincinnati, Ohio. My eyes skim over her details, but it's the answer to the question, "Why do you love the BDSM lifestyle?" that really grabs my attention. "I love the physical control and sexual dominance over the submissive," she writes. "It fills a need in me that nothing in the vanilla world can satisfy." The words spread more tingles over my body, a strange mix of fear and curiosity pooling in my gut. This woman knows exactly what she wants, and the thought of being on the receiving end of that desire both arouses and scares me. I swallow hard, torn between diving in and pulling back.

(7:24 pm) Reilly:
You're 44. That's so hot. I love older women. I'm 34. I've lightly explored D/s but my ex-girlfriend and I were amateurs.

(7:26 pm) Mistress MacKenzie:
I'm the real deal, Babygirl. Contracts, collars, safe words. Do you think you can handle that?

In my mind, I'm doing cartwheels. I can't believe this is actually happening. The surreal mix of thrill and disbelief floods my veins, and a surge of confidence fuels me. Go on, Reilly. Explore this side of yourself. For the first time in a while, I feel bold, daring even. With a deep breath, I type my response, ready to step further into this unknown part of myself, curious to see where it leads.

(7:28 pm) Reilly:
Yes, Mistress. I'm your girl.

(7:29 pm) Mistress MacKenzie:
Tell me what your kinks are.

I pause once again. I'm not really sure. Alexis and I never got that far—we dabbled a little, with her bossing me around, some blindfolds and handcuffs, but nothing beyond the basics. I quickly Google "types of kinks," my fingers trembling as I surf through pages, trying to figure out what stirs within me. After some inner contemplation, I finally respond.

(7:35 pm) Reilly:
Dominance and submission,
role playing, impact play
like spanking, age play.

(7:37 pm) Mistress MacKenzie:
Age play, huh? D/s …
I read your profile. You seem
pretty innocent. Want to be
my Babygirl, Princess, and I'll
be your Mommy Queen?

Yesssssss. That's exactly it. I feel that to my core. How did she know? It's like she's reading my mind, tapping into the thoughts I haven't ever admitted to myself. The thrill of being seen, understood, without saying a word—it's mesmerizing.

(7:39 pm) Reilly:
Yes! I want you to be
my Mommy Queen.

(7:40 pm) Mistress MacKenzie:
I will take care of you,
my good Babygirl. But
I will punish you when you
disobey me. Understand?

(7:41 pm) Reilly:
Yes, Mommy.
I can't believe how much fun I'm already having with this.

> (7:43 pm) Mistress MacKenzie:
> That's my good girl.
> I'll send you my contract,
> and if you consent to it all,
> you'll sign it and return it
> to me.

I give Mistress MacKenzie my email address, my mind buzzing with suspense as I wait for her to send this so-called "contract." A contract? Really? The word rolls around in my head, both strange and intriguing. What could possibly be so serious that it requires a formal agreement? My curiosity is piqued, and a slight nervousness creeps in as I wonder what kind of rules or boundaries I'm about to step into. Yet, despite the questions sweeping through my mind, I can't deny the excitement that accompanies the unknown.

Ding. My heart leaps as an email pops up at the top of my overflowing inbox. It's from MistressMacKenzieFemDom@gmail.com. I open the PDF attachment, and there it is, staring back at me in bold letters:

Mistress MacKenzie BDSM Contract

This contracted dated _______________ is the complete and entire agreement between the signatories. I, _________________, being of sound mind and body (hereinafter referred to as the "Domme"), and _________________, being of sound mind and body (hereinafter referred to as the "Sub"). The terms of this agreement will begin on _______________ and will remain in effect until one of the parties no longer wishes to participate. This contract shall also become null and void immediately upon request of the injured party following any breach of contract.

DOMME

1. Domme shall be responsible for keeping Sub safe at all times.
2. Domme will not allow or make Sub scene with any minors or animals at any time.
3. Domme will do everything within their power to train, educate, instruct, shape, and mold Sub into the best Sub possible.
4. Domme will receive pleasure from the activities outlined in clause three above.
5. Domme shall pick out the entire wardrobe of Sub when they are going out in public, however, Domme may instruct Sub to pick out said wardrobe and punish Sub for selecting an inappropriate outfit after Sub has received proper training on appropriate outfits for public display,
6. Domme shall read Sub's journal on a regular basis and agrees to not punish Sub for anything posted therein.
7. Domme shall request and honor the invocation of the safe word ("red=full stop, yellow=approaching my limit") by Sub.
8. Domme will stretch Sub's limit's to help Sub grow in life and position.

9. Domme will respect all hard limits of Sub.

10. Domme agrees to work with Sub on any new interests that Sub discovers.

11. Domme shall inform Sub of the reason for any punishment. Periodically during the punishment, Domme will remind Sub of the reason for the punishment although that can come from the Domme in the form of "Why are you being punished?" with an appropriate response from Sub.

12. Whereas Domme believes that family is important Domme will not keep Sub from staying in touch with their family and will not unreasonably withhold trips for Sub to visit their family.

13. Should the Domme allow Sub to scene with anyone, the Domme shall be present during the entire scene in order to assure that the Sub is unharmed and not forced to do anything on Sub's hard limit list.

SUB

1. Sub agrees to maintain body by regular bathing and all other routine body care (e.g. brushing teeth, etc.).

2. Sub shall maintain clean-shaven genitalia, legs, and armpits at all times unless instructed otherwise by Domme.

3. Sub agrees to study BDSM on a daily basis, including but not limited to searching the internet, reading books, attending BDSM munches, and/or other BDSM activities.

4. Sub shall journal daily including but not limited to thoughts, concerns, what was learned, and possible new interests to explore.

5. Sub agrees to accept any mark that Domme desires, anywhere on their body, indicating ownership by Domme.

6. Sub shall bring and show honor and respect to Domme at all times.

7. Sub agrees to never remove the ownership collar at any time.
8. Sub shall sit at the right foot of the Domme, whenever Domme is sitting, whenever and wherever feasible, if Domme requests.
9. Sub is not to wear any underwear unless necessary.
10. Sub will sleep naked.
11. Sub shall make themselves available for use by Domme in any way Domme desires at any time, when feasible, within the terms of this contract.
12. Sub shall not have any sexual contact at any time without permission from Domme.
13. Sub shall not orgasm without permission from Domme.
14. Sub shall not invoke the safe word unless absolutely necessary,
15. Sub shall count each stroke when being punished by flogging, caning, etc, and also must thank Domme following each stroke.

These terms are mutually agreed to by the affixing of the respective signatures below.

________________________________   ________________________________

Domme's Signature   Sub's Signature

________________________________   ________________________________

Date   Date

Holy shit. This is both exhilarating as fuck and dead-ass scary. I can't help but think of Fifty Shades of Grey, but this isn't some fictional fantasy—*this is fucking real*. My eyes skim over the contract, heart racing with every line, and then I go back and re-read certain parts just to be sure: "Domme will stretch Sub's limits," "Sub shall make themselves available for use by Domme," "Sub shall not orgasm without permission from Domme." Each word sends a jolt of electricity through me. I'm totally turned on, yet there's a pulse of fear mixed in, knowing this is about to get very real. It's one thing to fantasize about submission; it's another to see it spelled out in black and white, waiting for my consent.

But then I remind myself … this relationship will be a cyber relationship. Half of these rules won't even apply to me. The thought calms me slightly, a reminder that I'm still in control, even if the game says otherwise. With a deep breath, I sign the contract and email it back to Mistress MacKenzie. As I hit send, a swoosh of adrenaline surges through me. Part of me wonders just how far I'll let this go.

Mistress MacKenzie and I continue texting for the next hour, jumping headfirst into each other's lives and exploring this new dynamic between us. I learn she's a divorced woman with an adult son. She owns a crafting business, is a data entry clerk on the side … and she's also Mistress MacKenzie to three slaves and two sluts. Her favorite color? Red, of course. Her dream vacation? Greece. What's on her bucket list? Skydiving. Each new detail she shares pulls me further into her world, making this feel more real—and more thrilling. There's a magnetic pull between us, something I never expected but can't resist. Every response, every little reveal, feels like I'm stepping deeper into her orbit, and the more I learn, the more I want to know.

(7:57 pm) Mistress MacKenzie:

> I've got a task for you, Babygirl. Take a photo of all your toys and send it to me.

I love that she's taking initiative already. "Yes, Mommy," I respond. I send her a photo and get a positive heart emoji back.

(8:05 pm) Mistress MacKenzie:
Mmmhmm … maybe you're not as innocent as I think you are Baby.

Playing into the sexy flirting, I type back, "Just you wait and see, Mommy." It's 8:06 pm, and I'm having a blast, caught up in the playful, back-and-forth banter with Mistress MacKenzie. Then, it hits me—8:06 again? What is it with this number?

(8:10 pm) Mistress MacKenzie:
I've got an opportunity to run by you, my Babygirl. Please consider it.

(8:11 pm) Reilly:
Okay, Mommy Queen.

(8:13 pm) Mistress MacKenzie:
I've got an extra ticket to FatishCon. Huge fetish and kink convention in St. Petersburg, Florida. But … it's this weekend. Fri-Sat.

I'd love to meet you, take you around the convention, and maybe do some other fun stuff while we're there 😉 …

I freeze, my thoughts spiraling. Is she really asking me to fly to Florida, meet her at a convention, and stay with her in a hotel? Am I understanding this correctly? This is crazy. I can't just drop everything and go to Florida to meet a stranger. The thought alone is insane. I let several minutes pass, trying to make sense of this. My mind spins with questions and doubts, and I suddenly wish I had a glass of wine in my hand.

(8:18 pm) Mistress MacKenzie:
Hello? Are you still there?

I'm still trying to figure out how to respond. The truth is … I actually want to go. The idea of diving into this world with Mistress MacKenzie teaching me the ropes is exhilarating and almost irresistible. But fear holds me back, its grip tight and unrelenting. My heart aches with the conflict between what I want and what I'm scared to pursue.

(8:20 pm) Reilly:
That's really kind of you
to offer me the ticket, but I
can't just up and leave.
Plus, I barely know you.

There, that should end the conversation. Short, sweet, no bullshit. But as I hit send, an unexpected thrust of disappointment pulls at me. Why do I feel like I've just missed out on something? The tension in my chest lingers, a reminder that maybe, deep down, I was hoping for a different outcome.

(8:23 pm) Mistress MacKenzie:
Why do I have the feeling
that you actually want to go,
but you let fear take over?
You just spent the last hour

talking about how you've recently started to honor your desires and say "yes" to more opportunities that you otherwise would have never ventured to take. That you weren't scared, always-anxious Reilly anymore.

How is she picking up on my inner world so effortlessly?

(8:25 pm) Mistress MacKenzie:
I should have expected this.

(8:26 pm) Reilly:
What do you mean by that?

(8:29 pm) Mistress MacKenzie:
I knew you'd freak out and say "no." Babygirl, I know reaching out to me was a big step for you, and you should be proud of that—it shows you're serious about your journey of self-discovery. But now that you've made that first move, don't stop yourself short. You pride yourself on this year of personal development, but when it comes to honoring your deepest fantasies and exploring your curiosity, you're still holding back. How can you truly grow if you won't embrace every aspect of yourself— including your sexual desires?

She's right and she underestimates me. It's a feeling I know too well. My nervousness, my hesitation, the way I second-guess myself—it's all led people to make assumptions about me since I was a kid. People have seen my lack of confidence and concluded that I'm weak, incapable, or terrified. Maybe some of that is my own warped interpretation of people's perceived judgments, but those perceptions have left their mark, shaping how I've navigated the world. I've spent my life trying to prove myself over and over again—to teachers, coaches, co-workers, and even my parents—constantly working to show I'm more than the uncertainty they see on the surface.

The thought of having to prove myself one more time ignites something inside me. And in an instant, I'm shifted back in time, a memory of my junior high school basketball coach rushing to the forefront of my mind as if it never really left. His voice still echoes inside me, the frustration in his tone, the way he looked at me like I didn't belong on the court. That moment—one of many—still stings, but it also fuels me, reminding me of the fire that's been simmering beneath everyone's doubt all along …

Sweat pours down my face as my basketball teammates and I line up along the baseline, preparing for yet another round of brutal suicide sprints. The junior high gymnasium is a sweltering furnace on this balmy September evening; the industrial-sized fan perched uselessly on the stage might as well be blowing hot air. Coach Beckett is tearing into us, his voice bouncing off the walls, driven by the sharp pain of last night's 32-31 loss to Saxon Junior High. Apparently, these endless sprints are supposed to teach us the lesson: do better.

As the starting point guard, the weight of the loss feels like it's my fault. I had six assists but only three points, and I lost count of the turnovers. But the worst part? I missed the tying free throw. It's all I can think about as my legs burn with exhaustion and the sting of failure clings to me like a shadow.

Another grueling hour of practice drags on. Coach Beckett scrutinizes us Lady Mustangs as we scrimmage, his sharp eyes catching every misstep, every mistake. He's a coach of old-school tactics and brutal honesty—who cares that this is eighth-grade girls' basketball? Champions, as Billie Jean King so eloquently put it, keep playing until they get it right. The entire time, I can feel Coach's gaze boring into me, tracking every move, every decision, every outcome. With each passing minute, it seems like his blood boils a little hotter, his frustration simmering.

For what feels like the 30th time, I take the ball down the court, signaling a pick and roll. Just as we begin to execute the play, Coach's whistle pierces the air, cutting through the noise of the gym. "Reilly … get over here now!" he shouts, his voice laced with irritation.

My stomach drops as I sprint over to him. I stand before Coach, feeling the weight of my teammates' eyes on me, burning in my peripheral vision. He lowers himself just enough to get his face inches from mine, his breath hot with intensity.

"Punch me in the stomach!" he barks, his voice echoing through the gym.

What? Is he serious?

"Did you hear me? Punch me in the stomach!" he yells again, louder this time, his eyes locked onto mine, daring me.

I'm frozen, numb with shock and humiliation, the heat of embarrassment creeping up my neck as my teammates look on.

"Do you have what it takes? Show me you have fire in you! Punch me in the stomach!" he demands, his voice filled with a challenge that slices through my hesitation.

Paralyzed by fear, I just stare back at Coach Beckett, my mind racing. The whispers of my teammates swirl around me, adding to the pressure, as I stand there, freaked out and grossed out. If I don't punch him, I'll be underestimated. That's exactly the lesson he's driving home.

Deep down, I want to do it—to show him I'm not a coward.

Staring into Coach's piercing eyes, I take a deep breath, pull my arm back, and drive my fist straight into his gut with everything I've got. The shock on his face is immediate. I actually hit him—hard.

He doesn't flinch, doesn't step back. Instead, he yells, "Again!" The command is sharp and unyielding. Without thinking, I wind up and punch him a second time.

I snap back to the present moment, the memory of that day still vivid, but somehow, it feels different now—like a weird nightmare that's finally starting to make sense. That moment with Coach Beckett has haunted me into my adult life, a reminder of the times I've been minimized. But now, in this moment of clarity, I realize something: I actually accomplished the crazy thing he demanded of me—the thing he thought I couldn't do.

I let out a sigh. It's time to shift my perspective. It's not about constantly feeling underestimated. It's about embracing the courage to be unafraid, to face challenges head-on, and prove, not to others, but to myself, that I'm stronger than they think.

(8:35 pm) Reilly:
Friday and Saturday, huh?

(8:36 pm) Mistress MacKenzie:
Babygirl, are you having a change of heart?

(8:37 pm) Reilly:
I'll do it. I'll meet you there this weekend.

Oddly, I feel calm. I'm going to do this. Holy shit.

(8:38 pm) Mistress MacKenzie:
That's my good baby! Book your flights now. I'm staying at the Hilton St. Petersburg Bayfront Hotel.

The plan quickly takes shape. Friday, I'll take a personal day off from work. I'll catch an early flight to Florida, meet Mistress MacKenzie in the hotel lobby, and step into this adventure with bells on. By midday Saturday, I'll be on a plane back home. Like that night in Japan, this is just another moment where I take control of my desires—no hesitation, just confidence and action.

(8:55 pm) Reilly:
Mommy Queen, my flights are booked. I should be at the hotel on Friday around 1:00 pm. I'll message you when I arrive.

I feel good. I feel invigorated. This is me doing something courageous, stepping out of my comfort zone. I'm not afraid to take chances and put myself first. Envisioning the convention, I have no idea what to expect, but that only fuels my anticipation. The thought of what's to come sends fireworks through me. And as for Mistress MacKenzie … I can't wait to get my hands on her.

(8:57 pm) Mistress MacKenzie:
Get ready, Babygirl, for the best fuck of your life.

CHAPTER 15
epic

My Uber glides to a stop beneath the hotel's grand portico, the sound of the engine humming as I slide out, gripping my overnight suitcase and backpack like lifelines. I stand there for a moment, rooted to the spot, my heart pounding as my eyes lock onto the hotel's gleaming revolving door. The Uber pulls away, leaving behind a screech of tires on the pavement—and with it, any chance of turning back. Reality hits hard—I'm moments away from meeting Mistress MacKenzie face-to-face. Just four days ago, she was a stranger I met online. Now, I'm about to cross into her world. My breath catches as I push through the revolving door, stepping into the lobby where the bold signs for FetishCon dominate every corner, drawing me deeper into the unknown.

FetishCon
Friday and Saturday
Cypress and Sunset Ballrooms
Must Be 21+

I find a seat on a sleek bench near a softly bubbling water fountain, the gentle sound doing little to calm the rush of nerves swirling inside me. I send a quick message to Mistress MacKenzie to let her know I've arrived, my fingers gliding over the screen, a restless thrill pulsing beneath the surface. I describe myself: jeans, a plaid shirt, and a backward trucker hat—an odd contrast in a lobby full of women drifting by in tropical-colored sundresses. Hard to miss me. My mind flickers to Mistress MacKenzie's profile photos—long blonde hair cascading over her shoulders, a petite frame, and that tattoo sleeve on her right arm, vivid against her tan skin. I wonder if she'll look just like her pictures, or if meeting in person will feel different, more intense.

As I wait for her response, I run my fingers through my hair, the motion repetitive, almost soothing. I pop a mint into my mouth, and reposition my hat, tugging it down like a shield. Glancing at my reflection in the nearby window, the anxious energy is written all over my face—wide eyes, slightly parted lips, the flush of nervous anticipation. Calling it jitters would be an understatement.

Five minutes stretch on, each second dragging longer than the last. Then, without warning, gentle hands glide onto my shoulders, the touch soft but intentional, sending a shockwave through me. They slide down my arms, slow and deliberate, as if savoring every inch. Before I can react, a quiet, seductive voice whispers against my ear, warm breath caressing my skin. "I've been waiting for you, Babygirl," Mistress MacKenzie murmurs, the words sending vibrations straight to my core.

Fuck. Arousal hits me, heat rising fast and fierce within me, making my pulse quicken. I turn around, and there she is—Mistress MacKenzie, breathtaking, like a perfect blend of Marilyn Monroe and 1990s Pamela Anderson. Strikingly gorgeous. She's dressed in skin-tight black pants and a figure-hugging purple shirt, showing off the fullness of her breasts. Her wavy blonde hair falls perfectly across her face, catching in the breeze that drifts through the open windows of the hotel lobby. The moment feels cinematic, almost unreal as if she's stepping straight out of a dream and into my reality.

"Hi. It's so wonderful to meet you." I say.

"Right back at ya, Babygirl. Now try that introduction once again," says Mistress MacKenzie a bit sternly, but seductively.

Dammit. I've already pissed her off. What did I do wrong? I stare at her perplexed. She raises one eyebrow and tilts her head to look me squarely in the eyes. *Oh, I know what she wants.*

"Hi. It's so wonderful to meet you, *Mommy Queen.*" I say with emphasis on Mommy Queen.

"That's my good girl." Mistress MacKenzie replies. "You must always address me as Mommy or Mommy Queen when you're in my presence."

"Or what? I'll be punished?" I respond teasingly, already feeling relaxed enough to get into my submissive character.

"Every time you disobey me today, naughty girl, I will discipline you tonight." Mistress MacKenzie says suggestively. "Do you understand, Baby?"

Clearly, Mistress MacKenzie is already in character. "Let's put your suitcase in my room, and then hit the convention," she says calmly, breathy.

I grab my rolling suitcase, sling on my backpack, and follow Mistress MacKenzie to the elevators, already feeling like I'm at her mercy. The anticipation is electric, crackling in the air between us. Room 806 … seriously … what the hell? The "Do Not Disturb" sign is dangling from the outside handle, a clear message that this space is entirely ours. She opens the door with a smooth swipe of her key, and as we step inside, I immediately notice the drawn shades, casting the room in a dim, intimate light.

The room has been transformed into a dungeon-like feel. There are different types of whips hanging in the closet, handcuffs on each bedpost, and an array of dildos and vibrators of all shapes and sizes on the entertainment unit—not to forget nipple clamps, Ben Wa balls, and butt plugs of all kinds.

"Welcome to Mistress MacKenzie's playroom, Babygirl." she says as she grabs me by the waist and pushes me down on the bed, her body on top of mine.

I am in ecstasy playing out my fantasy in real life with this bombshell, gorgeous woman. I go to kiss her but Mistress MacKenzie pulls away. "Not yet, Baby. You have to earn the kiss of my lips … both of them." she says alluringly.

Can she get any fucking hotter?

"Let's go check out this convention, Mommy," I say assuredly.

"Yes, Babygirl. Let's do that. But first, you must put on this collar," Mistress MacKenzie says. "Tonight, I own you." I grab the collar from her hands—it's a black leather band with a silver heart in the middle. Adjusting my plaid, button-down shirt, I get the collar secured around my neck. "Now, people will know you're mine, Baby."

Inside the Cypress and Sunset Ballrooms, I'm struck with sheer astonishment at the vibrant energy and atmosphere that surrounds me. It's like stepping into a different world. Hundreds of booths stretch out before me, each one offering something tantalizing—BDSM toys, lingerie, books, movies, coaching sessions, boot camps, and group trips. The air is thick with excitement, a mix of curiosity and desire.

In the corners of the ballrooms, live exhibitions captivate the event guests. On one stage, a BDSM fashion show is in full swing, showcasing the latest in provocative lingerie. On another, a dominatrix expertly practices whipping techniques on her submissive partner, each crack of the whip reverberating through the space. Strobe lights pulse and flash, adding a sense of urgency and intensity to the conjoined ballrooms. An erotic and sensual promo video plays on a loop on a giant Jumbotron, drawing eyes and setting the tone. It's like a BDSM adventure zone in here, every corner brimming with possibility and exploration.

I think of Alexis—she has no idea I'm here. The thought of how she'd react brings a sly smile to my face. She'd lose her mind in a place like this—vendors everywhere, entertainment at every turn, and merchandise that would make her eyes light up. Unable to resist, I snap a photo of the venue, capturing the pulse and energy of the scene. With a hint of mischief, I text it to her with the message, "You'll never guess where I am." She responds.

(1:23 pm) Alexis:
Where the fuck R U?

(1:24 pm) Reilly:
I'm in Florida at a kink convention

(1:25 pm) Alexis:
What?! ‼️

(1:26 pm) Reilly:
You'll never guess how I ended up here

(1:27 am) Alexis:
How?

(1:27 pm) Reilly:
I met a femme domme on a kink app and we decided to meet here at this event 😜

(1:27 pm) Alexis:
Oh …

(1:28 pm) Reilly:
Can't wait to tell you all about it. Gotta go. TTYL

Mistress MacKenzie gives me another stern look indicating I need to put my phone away. "Sorry, Mommy."

"You've already got two spankings so far tonight, Babygirl." Mistress MacKenzie says with a grin on her face.

For the next four hours, we explore every inch of the convention, visiting every booth, chatting with nearly every vendor, and soaking in all the live exhibitions we can. Mistress MacKenzie leads the way with confidence, and I follow close beside her, sticking to her like an obedient puppy dog. She runs into some friends and previous mentors along the way, exchanging knowing glances and inside jokes that I can only guess at. The entire time, I stay right by her side, feeling the thrill of being under her guidance and control in this electrifying world.

Mistress MacKenzie tantalizes me throughout the day. In a booth selling glass dildos, she comes up behind me and sticks her hand down my jeans, and whispers "Have you ever fucked yourself with an ice dildo, Babygirl?" And while browsing a booth selling bondage equipment, Mistress MacKenzie tells me she is an experienced rope bunny.

My body is electric with tingles. I can't wait to get up to the hotel room … and stay there for the rest of the night.

"Babygirl, I think we've seen everything. And I don't want you getting too tired on me. We have a long night ahead of us." Mistress MacKenzie says sexy as hell.

"Mommy, I'm ready to go upstairs and play," I say.

"Yes, let's go, Baby," she replies as we start walking toward the exit.

Back in Mistress MacKenzie's hotel room, there's no time for hesitation. The moment the door closes, her voice cuts through the air with authority. "Take off your shirt and kneel beside me." My hands fumble for only a second before I obey, sinking to the floor. Cold metal of handcuffs snaps around my wrists and the bedpost, securing me in place. "Sit there like a good girl while I slip into something a little more suited to your desires," she purrs before disappearing into the bathroom. I'm left alone, surrounded by the soft glow of flickering fake candles, their light dancing against the walls, casting shadows that only heighten the eroticism curling through me.

She walks out seductively in a leather bondage suit and high heels— every curve of her body accentuated. I can smell her perfume from across the room—its sweet scent putting me under a spell. Mistress MacKenzie approaches me with her whip.

"I need to punish you, Babygirl, for the naughty things you did earlier today," she says sternly.

"Yes, Mommy Queen," I reply sheepishly.

She cracks the whip against my backside as I try to hold in the pain. "Thank you, Mommy," I say per the rules of our contract. She strikes again. "Thank you, Mommy," I repeat. She takes off the handcuffs and pulls me into her arms.

"I'm sorry, Baby, that I had to be so mean," Mistress McKenzie says intimately, her voice dripping with authority. "But I trust you've learned your lesson. Now, worship my pussy like a good girl." Her command ignites a fire between us, and the night unfolds in a symphony of indulgence. We explore each other's desires with unrelenting passion, teasing with toys, experimenting with every angle of pleasure, and finally surrendering to the warmth of the room's luxurious, oversized bathtub, where the boundaries of control and devotion blur completely.

The night unfolds like a fever dream—surreal, intoxicating, and unforgettable. It's not just the physical intensity that leaves me breathless—it's the raw power of giving in, of embracing my deepest desires. By the time the sun begins to rise, I know this night will leave an indelible mark—a vivid, searing memory of bliss and release.

At the airport the next day, I can't stop smiling. A charge courses through me—I feel exhilarated, proud even, for embracing my decision to fly to Florida for a night of reckless abandon. But as the buzz of last night lingers, Alexis sneaks back into my thoughts, and the edges of my smile begin to fade. Her response to my quick text yesterday gnaws at me. She didn't seem excited for me, not like I'd hoped. I didn't get to share much, but her simple "Oh" felt heavier than it should have, a weight I wasn't expecting. The uncertainty tightens within me, and I decide to reach out while waiting at my gate.

(1:43 pm) Reilly:

Hey. I'm on my way back home. Last night was EPIC ⭐

Unlike Alexis, who is usually quick to respond, there's silence—30 minutes and still nothing. With each passing minute, the knot in my stomach tightens, twisting a little more, doubt creeping in like an unwelcome guest. My phone feels heavier in my hand, every second amplifying my uneasiness. What could be keeping her from replying?

(2:13 pm) Alexis:
That's cool.

That's it? That's all she's got to say? The message stares back at me, as empty as it feels. Two words—barely enough to scratch the surface of everything I thought we were building as rekindled friends. I carry on anyways.

(2:14 pm) Reilly:
Her name was Mistress MacKenzie and she was my Mommy and I was her Babygirl. I discovered my kink and omg, it felt so good.

(2:17 pm) Alexis:
Happy for you.

Alexis is being short with me. Something's definitely up. My mind races—did I offend her somehow? Does she disapprove of me meeting up with a stranger? The more I think about it, the more unsettled I feel. Her usual warmth is missing, replaced by something cold and distant. And now, the silence between us feels thick, as if there's more she's not saying.

(2:19 pm) Reilly:

> I sense something's off. I'm about to board my flight. Can you please tell me what's on your mind?

I wait patiently for her response—but nothing. Boarding starts, passengers filter in, and soon the entire plane is loaded. The flight attendants move through the aisles, performing their final safety checks, their voices barely registering as I stare at my phone, hoping for a last-minute message. But, nothing. With a heavy sigh, I power down my phone. Disappointment settles in as the airplane engines hum to life.

Two hours later, I arrive back in New York City. The moment the plane touches down, I power my phone back on, anxious to see if anything has changed. A notification pings and my heart skips a beat—there's a text waiting for me. My fingers hover for a second, nerves buzzing under my skin. I click it open, a tight knot forming in my stomach, fearful of what I'm about to read.

(3:02 pm) Alexis:

> I don't like that you hooked up with someone else. I'm developing real feelings for you, Reilly. It's been on my mind, and I can't shake it. Can we talk?

The words stop me cold, freezing my thoughts as they sink in. My breath catches in my throat as I stare at the screen, reading the message over and over. It's everything I didn't expect and yet feared all at once. Alexis has feelings for me—real feelings. The kind she swore would never happen. And now, after everything, I'm left to process the weight of her words, unsure of what to feel or how to respond.

As I wait my turn to exit the airplane, I'm suddenly hit with a harsh flashback to the night I told Alexis I had real feelings for her. There was awkward fidgeting, stumbling words, my nervous laugh when I panicked … it all comes rushing back to the forefront of my mind …

It's Halloween night, and Alexis and I are at our friend's Boo Bash, sipping Black Magic Margaritas and turning heads in our matching costumes—she's the sexy cheerleader, and I'm the hot jock. As the party swirls around us, my mind is consumed by two things: getting back to Alexis's apartment and tearing that cheerleader's costume off her, and finally confessing my real feelings for her. I can't shake the hope that tonight might be the turning point, where we leave the friends-with-benefits label behind and step into something deeper, something meaningful.

I've been on edge all evening—hovering around Alexis, waiting on her hand and foot, barely leaving her side. I can tell she senses something is off, though she hasn't said anything yet. My stomach is in knots as I suggest we step outside for some air. The crisp fall breeze greets us as we walk into our friend's backyard, the full moon hanging overhead, casting a soft glow over the city. It's the perfect Halloween night—cool and clear, with the distant sound of kids' laughter echoing through the neighborhood. I glance at Alexis, her face illuminated by the moonlight, and I know the moment to confess is closing in.

I bend down, pick up a fallen leaf, and start fidgeting with it like a nervous child, twisting the stem between my fingers. My eyes dart to Alexis, and I can't help but let out a few nervous giggles, trying to gather my thoughts.

"Do you want to tell me something, Reilly?" Alexis asks, her voice edged with confusion, her eyes searching mine.

"Um … yes … I do." I stammer, a little taken aback by the shift in her tone, her sternness catching me off guard. "Here's the thing …"

"Oh my God … you're ending things, aren't you?" she blurts out, her voice cracking with fear. Her eyes, wide and searching, fill with panic as if she's bracing for a blow that's about to land.

"What? No, no, absolutely not!" I rush to reassure her, shaking my head emphatically. "That's the last thing I want." I step closer, my heart pounding. "Alexis, I want more than this … more than just friends-with-benefits. I want to be a real couple. I've fallen for you—hard—and I need you to know that. I have real feelings for you."

A heavy silence settles between us, thickening the air. Alexis looks unnerved, her expression unreadable, and the tension in the space around us becomes suffocating. This is not the reaction I'd hoped for. A lump forms in my throat as the weight of her silence sinks in, and tears start welling in my eyes, threatening to spill over.

"I guess it's just me, then … isn't it?" I whisper, the sting of embarrassment creeping into my voice. I look down, my heart sinking as the vulnerability of the moment crashes over me.

"Reilly, I'm just not looking to take things any further," Alexis says gently, her voice steady but firm. "Don't get me wrong, I love what we have. But we both agreed when this started … it was about fun, no strings attached." Her words hit like a slow, painful echo.

I feel heartbroken. The air leaves my lungs, and the heaviness of her reminder lands hard with a thud, crushing the hope I'd built up.

"What we have is perfect just the way it is," Alexis continues, her tone casual, almost indifferent. "Great sex, lots of fun … and no commitment. I'm not looking for anything serious, Reilly. I like the freedom of not being tied down. And I thought that's where you were, too." Her words dangle in the air, a stark contrast to the openness I had just laid bare.

"Well, I've caught feelings for you," I admit, my voice softening. "I didn't plan for this to happen." I take a breath, searching her eyes for any flicker of understanding. "I mean, we practically act like a couple, don't you think? It's not just great sex—there's more here. The chemistry between us is undeniable. We have amazing conversations, we do all these fun things together … it's gone way beyond the bedroom for me."

"I'm flattered, Reilly. You're always so sweet," Alexis says with a soft smile, her tone kind but distant. "Thank you for being honest with me, truly. But … I just don't feel the same way. I don't have those kinds of *feelings." She pauses, her eyes pleading. "But please, don't let this ruin what we have together. I can't lose you."*

I snap back to reality as it's my turn to step off the plane. The shift in my life feels surreal. Now, the tables have turned—Alexis has feelings for me, but I'm no longer in that same place anymore. If this self-imposed year of no dating has taught me anything, it's that I no longer need someone else's validation to feel complete. I'm learning to trust myself, honor my boundaries, and embrace my own worth. This journey isn't about finding love—or maybe, in a way, it is. *Self-love.*

I stop walking in the airport, Alexis's last text flashing through my mind: "I don't like that you hooked up with someone else. I'm developing real feelings for you." The weight of those words press down on me. Rather than taking the easy way out with a text, I decide to call her.

"Hey there," Alexis answers, her voice familiar, tinged with a cautious edge.

"Hi, Alexis," I say, steadying myself, aiming for calm confidence. "I figured a call would be better than texting. Thank you for being honest about your feelings. The thing is … I'm not in the same place I was when we were together. I've spent a lot of time looking inward, and I think, right now, the person I need to fall in love with … is myself. But I don't want this to ruin what we've been rebuilding. Just like you told me last Halloween when I stood there spilling my heart out … I can't lose you."

Alexis is silent for a few seconds. "Alright, Reilly. If that's where you are, I have to respect that." The call ends, and I realize I've been standing in front of Patsy's Pizzeria—the airport branch, of all places. I feel the irony, given that it's always been *our* spot. A part of me wonders—will this be the end for us? Or is there more to come? Why do I always find myself anticipating more chapters between us as if our story isn't quite over yet?

CHAPTER 16
quinny-girl

May has arrived, the city is in full bloom, drenched in sunshine and buzzing with the promise of summer. Next month marks the culmination of my year-long hiatus of no dating—a year spent sorting through past baggage, embracing a more confident version of myself, and carving a healthier path forward.

I've conquered my battle with alcohol. I've broken my shell and stepped into self-assurance. I've started a path forward with my sister. I've let go of feelings of self-doubt. I've discovered my spirituality. Each step of progress is bringing me closer to the truest version of who I want to be. And with my 35th birthday just around the corner, the timing couldn't feel more fitting.

Standing in my kitchen, heating up leftover lasagna from last night, I ponder. The end of this experiment deserves a crescendo, a grand finale that marks the close of something so transformative. But what would that even look like? What kind of moment could capture the significance of this year and everything it's come to mean to me? Feeling a sudden surge of inspiration, I head into my home office on this beautiful late Saturday afternoon and pull up the novel I've been working on for several months. I scroll back to the beginning and start reading—immersing myself in every word, refining each sentence, adjusting the flow until each paragraph feels just right. With each revision, it's as if I'm pouring my growth and experiences into every line.

I pause, letting a subtle sense of fulfillment settle in as I consider the direction this book is taking. Leaning back in my chair, I stretch out, hands resting behind my head, feet propped on the ottoman. The room holds a comfortable stillness, and for once, I'm simply content in this quiet moment, letting the satisfaction of perseverance sink in.

I hear Quinn tiptoe toward my office, the faint creak of the wooden floors giving her away. When I glance up, the sight of her catches me off guard—her usual bubbly smile is nowhere to be found. Instead, a rare seriousness darkens her face, a look I'm not used to seeing on my always-cheerful little girl.

"Hey, Quinny-girl," I say, giving her a soft smile, hoping to lift the mood. "Did you finish reading your book for school? How about we go grab snow cones from Polar Paradise? I could use a little sugar." I glance at my watch. "It's 6:08 … how about we leave at 6:15."

Good God. There it is again—this time it's 608 instead of 806 … but it's the same numbers, just backward. It's like this set of numbers is following me, showing up everywhere I turn.

"I'm good, Mom. But I need to talk to you about something," Quinn says, her tone steady and uncharacteristically serious.

"Okay," I respond as I motion her to the sofa. "Come in and sit down."

Quinn takes a deep breath, her expression unreadable. "I don't want to go to basketball camp this summer—or ever again, actually." Her words land with a subdued finality, the kind that feels like a door softly closing.

"Ever?" I ask, completely taken aback. Basketball has been her whole world. "Okay, hon … What do you want to do instead?" I have a hunch what she's going to say.

"I've been hinting for a while now … I want to take acting and modeling classes," Quinn says, her voice edging into a slight whine. "It's my number one wish, Mom. And Tessa says that if I have any chance of "making it big," I've got to start now."

I glance down at my shoes as if they might somehow provide the answers I can't find. Disappointment seeps through me. I've been against this from the start—acting and modeling school always felt like such a scam with the outrageous fees and constant rejection. It'll crush her. What are the odds she's actually going to "make it big"? As for basketball, she's an incredible athlete, and now she's ready to just throw it all away.

"Quinny-girl, my answer has always been "no," and I'm not changing it," I say, my voice steady but heavy with disappointment. "Acting and modeling is a full-time commitment, and that would mean giving up basketball completely. Basketball is where you shine—it's what you're meant to do."

"But, Mom …" Quinn's voice edges toward desperation, her eyes wide with emotion. "I don't want to do basketball anymore. It's not what I want."

"Quinn, you don't know what you want. You think you do, but you don't. You're a star athlete, and basketball has been your passion since you were two. Acting and modeling? You've never even shown interest in that until recently." My words come out sharper than I intended, and a wave of guilt hits me as I realize I might be crushing her dreams.

"Mom … please …" Quinn begs, her voice trembling, her eyes searching mine, pleading with me to reconsider.

"My answer is no, Quinn. End of story," I say, my voice firm.

Quinn's face crumples, her heartbreak written across her features as she turns and rushes to her bedroom, tears streaming down her cheeks. The door slams, the sound echoing through the apartment, leaving me frozen in place. Why am I so determined to keep her in basketball, even when she's telling me it's no longer what she wants? It feels like I'm forcing her into a mold that no longer fits, pushing her to be someone she's outgrown—and I hate myself for it.

I need help navigating this. I should probably talk to Connor—but I already know he'll be just as disappointed as I am that Quinn doesn't want to play basketball anymore. I'll deal with that later. Right now, I know who I really want to talk to … Alexis. I've been giving her space since she told me about her feelings, letting things settle. But maybe this conversation will help break the silence between us, and ease the awkwardness that's been lingering since then.

(6:41 pm) Reilly:

You busy? Quinn just
dropped a bomb on me,
and I really need your help.
Or at least your perspective.

(6:43 pm) Alexis:

Okay, sure. Lay it on me,
what's going on?

I quickly summarize the conversation, hitting the main points—Quinn's sudden decision to quit basketball, her desire to pursue acting and modeling, and the argument that followed. I don't hold back, sharing my confusion, frustration, and the guilt that's been gnawing at me since the door slammed.

(6:52 pm) Alexis:

Reilly, I'll be honest with you—
I think you're off base on this one.

You, more than anyone, know
what's it's like to live behind
a mask, to play a part that
doesn't reflect who you really
are at your core.

The realization hits me hard. Alexis is right—completely right. From the day Quinn was born, wasn't I the one who swore I'd always let her live her truth? Who am I to stand in the way of her exploring her own passions, just because they don't fit the vision I had for her?

(6:55 pm) Reilly:

You're totally right.

Caught up in the moment, I type, "This is why I love you." The words appear on the screen before I can stop them.

(6:57 pm) Alexis:

Happy to be here from you.

Reflecting on Alexis's wise words, my mind spins like a roulette wheel. I know exactly how Quinn's feeling—what it's like to have a parent who doesn't fully support you, to feel trapped inside someone else's expectations. The roulette wheel stops, and I think about the repercussions I experienced when I told Dad I was gay.

When I told him two years ago, he didn't take it well—at all. We didn't speak for months. He even missed Quinn's basketball championship game because he couldn't bear to see me. When we finally broke the silence, he confessed to feeling angry, confused, and irritated—frustrated that he had another "different" kind of child. The sting of those words still lingers, a sharp reminder of what it feels like to face rejection from the one person who's supposed to love you unconditionally. But then something amazing happened during last year's Pride Month.

In my mind, I'm transported back to last June, sitting at a small table for two at P&G's in my hometown, waiting for Dad. Just the two of us for lunch—nothing unusual, or so I thought. Little did I know how much would shift in that single afternoon.

The scent of charred cheeseburgers and freshly poured beer wafts through the air, blending with the low hum of conversation from the bar. Dad's usually right on time, but today he's five minutes late. I sit there patiently, sipping my Bloody Mary, the salt on the rim tangling with the bitterness of the drink. We don't get much daddy-daughter time these days, so this feels like a rare treat—even with the usual undercurrent of nerves buzzing beneath my skin.

I drove back home to reconnect with old high school friends and attend my hometown's Pride Parade. It still feels surreal that I'm out of the closet. My mind drifts back to those years I spent drowning in unhappiness, pretending to be someone I wasn't. I think about that night in college when I almost ended it all—the struggles with alcohol, the constant anxiety, the gnawing pit in my stomach from living a lie. But now, here I am, out and proud—celebrating the real Reilly in the very place where all the pain began.

The pub's front door squeaks open, and the bells jangle softly as Dad steps inside. The sunlight streaming through the entrance casts him in silhouette, making him almost a shadowy figure. I wave him over to the table, and without hesitation, he heads my way.

As he gets closer, his tall, lean frame and that slow, familiar glide come into focus—classic Dad. Just then, something catches my eye. I blink, unsure if I'm seeing it right.

He's wearing a Gay Pride t-shirt.

I blink again as if my eyes are playing tricks on me. But no—there it is, a big Pride flag across his chest with the words "Proud Ally" underneath. The last thing I ever expected to see on Dad.

Howie barks from the other room and I snap back to the present. That moment remains one of the proudest of my life. Seeing Dad in that t-shirt was more than a gesture—it was a symbol of how far he'd come in his acceptance of me. And now, each June he proudly wears that shirt to show his unwavering support for me.

My thoughts drift back to Quinn. Guilt oozing out of me. As a parent, I owe her the same level of support Dad eventually gave me. No matter what she chooses in life, she deserves to feel seen, just as I do now.

I walk to Quinn's bedroom and gently knock on the door. "Quinn, can you open up, please? I really want to talk some more," I say, keeping my voice calm and reassuring. Hoping she senses my genuineness.

She slowly cracks the door open, and I step inside, settling onto her bed. My eyes meander to the shelves lined with her basketball trophies and medals, each one a reminder of the life she's built around the sport. When I turn back to her, our eyes lock—just like the day she was born. Her intensity is undeniable, and I can feel the weight of the moment pressing between us as if she's waiting for me to say the one thing that will make this right.

"Quinny-girl …" I begin, my voice gentle. "I'm not going to stand in the way of you pursuing your dreams. I want you to do whatever makes you happy—whether that's acting, basketball, or underwater basket-weaving," I say with a small laugh, trying to ease the tension. "What matters to me is that you follow your heart and become the person you're meant to be. If acting and modeling classes are what you want, follow your heart's desires. No one should stop you from your dreams."

Tears of joy well up in Quinn's eyes as she leans in, wrapping her arms around me tightly. Her embrace feels full of the emotions she's been holding back, and in this moment, I know she feels heard and understood.

"I'm 100 percent behind you, always and forever," I whisper, holding her close, letting her feel the certainty in my words.

CHAPTER 17
hypnosis

The sharp ring of my alarm clock jolts me awake, fragments of a lucid dream dancing before me. Then I realize, it's my birthday—30-fucking-five. I rub the sleep out of my eyes and give Howie some morning snuggles. Outside, the distant rumble of thunder echoes through the city as gentle rain pitter-patters against my window on this quiet June morning.

For the past few months, my vibrant dreams have left me both mesmerized and unsettled. My budding spirituality makes me feel as though they're offering cryptic glimpses into my past lives, patchy pieces of a larger puzzle waiting to be understood. Or maybe I'm just more conscious of everything now.

Take, for instance, the recurring dream I have about losing the ability to run or walk—living a life where my body betrays me, trapping me in stillness. Other times, I'm in an airplane, reliving the moments just before a catastrophic crash.

I reach for my phone, curious to see who's remembered my birthday so far. One message lights up the screen—just one—and, of course, it's from Alexis. Steady, reliable Alexis, who never misses a date or milestone. I pause, feeling a flicker of appreciation.

(7:57 am) Alexis:

🎉 Happy Birthday, you fabulous human! 🎉 May today be filled with cake, confetti, and all the good vibes! P.S. Don't forget to tell everyone you're 25 again 😉

I let out a chuckle. Alexis seems remarkably at ease with everything. I text back.

(9:08 am) Reilly:

Thank u! Lol … when did we get so old??

(9:10 am) Alexis:

Are we like middle age now??

(9:11 am) Reilly:

No! We've got at least 5 more years b4 that!

(9:13 am) Alexis:

What are you doing on your special day?

(9:14 am) Reilly:

I took the day off work! And cuz my year of dedicated self-exploration comes to an end this week, my bday present to myself is a session with a past life regression hypnotherapist today … to hopefully unlock shit about my past lives. I'm fucking excited!! 😁

(9:15 am) Alexis:
Wow, intense! Have a good time with that … I guess lol

The rich aroma of freshly brewed coffee pulls me out of bed. I slip into my favorite flannel pajama bottoms and a white tank top, savoring the cool air against my skin—there's something so freeing about sleeping naked. As I pad into the kitchen, I wonder if I've grown a little too comfortable with this no-dating thing—relishing the freedom of doing whatever the hell I please. Outside, the storm is lifting, and faint beams of sunlight spill through the windows, breathing life into the space. Feeling a surge of energy, I grab my phone and text Alexis again.

(9:53am) Reilly:
What are you up to after 3? Want to go kayaking on the Hudson?

(9:55am) Alexis:
Yeah, that sounds great

(9:57am) Reilly:
Meet you at Pier 84 at 3 👍

At 11:25 am, my Uber pulls up to the NYC Past Life Hypnosis Center in the heart of Chelsea, Manhattan. A knot of anxiety tightens in my chest as I step out, knowing I'm about to be hypnotized and glimpse pieces of my past lives. After checking in at the front desk, I sit in the cozy waiting area, excited to unlock hints of who I was before I was Reilly. A faux fireplace flickers gently in the corner, casting a soft glow over the room, while the calming notes of Mozart and Chopin fill the air, offering a momentary reprieve from the weight of what's to come. I take a deep breath, wondering what truths I'll uncover as I wait for Catherine, my hypnotherapist, to appear.

"Reilly, welcome. I hope you found us alright," a soft voice calls from the side door. I glance up to see Catherine—tall, effortlessly stunning, dressed in tailored khaki pants, a crisp navy collared shirt tucked neatly into a brown belt, with perfectly matched shoes. Of course, my past life regression hypnotherapist has to be gorgeous. As if delving into the secrets of my past lives wasn't intimidating enough, now I have to do it while trying to keep my cool in front of her.

She guides me into her office, where I settle into the soft embrace of her plush sofa. "We'll start with a conversation," Catherine begins, her voice calm and practiced. "I like to get to know my clients first—explore any specific issues, questions, or reasons you have for diving into your past lives. This might mean discussing current life challenges, relationships, recurring patterns, or even emotions that feel unexplainable." Her tone is reassuring, with the ease of someone who's done this countless times before.

I jump in with pure naivety. "I came out as a lesbian two years ago, after a lifetime of denying my sexuality. But even though I had fully embraced my identity, by this time last year, I still felt a deep disconnect from my true self," I proclaim.

"So I committed to a year of no dating—as dating was my biggest distraction to focusing on me. Over the past 12 months, I've unearthed old wounds, tackled bad habits, explored my spirituality, and analyzed myself on deeper levels."

"The concept of past lives intrigues me … I believe in reincarnation," I say enthusiastically. "Today, I'm here to peek into those past lives, to uncover any connections that shape who I am today. I want to make sense of the events in my life today and gain a clearer understanding of my true essence, at the soul level."

Catherine smiles warmly. "You're definitely ready. You're at a perfect point in your self-exploration journey to start uncovering your past lives."

"Are you ready to begin?" Catherine asks, her voice steady and calm.

"Let's do it," I reply, feeling a mix of excitement and nerves.

"You can stay seated or lie down if that's more comfortable," she says, her tone nurturing. "The key is to relax as much as possible. Now, close your eyes and take three deep, slow breaths."

Catherine plays soft, melodic music in the background—loud enough to quaintly fill the room with a gentle ambiance but quiet enough to tune out.

"As you are, let your body melt into complete relaxation. Soften the muscles in your face … relax your eyes … your mouth … your jaw … let your tongue rest … release the tension in your shoulders … your arms … your hands … feel the ease spreading through your chest and back …" Catherine's voice flows slowly, guiding me deeper into stillness. Gradually, my body succumbs to a serene weightlessness, and my mind clears, free from the usual train of speeding thoughts.

"Simply be. As your body continues to soften, breathe naturally. With each inhale, feel your body sink deeper into relaxation, and with every exhale, let go of the stresses of the day."

"Now, imagine yourself floating gently down a river of multicolored light, each hue glowing softly around you. You drift effortlessly, the current slow and graceful, as the light lifts you higher and higher, wrapping you in a protective bubble. From this vantage, you can see the whole earth beneath you. Inside this bubble, you are completely safe, filled with divine wisdom. You are fully at ease, fully relaxed, and embraced by a profound sense of peace. This bubble nourishes both your mind and soul. All you need to do is breathe … and simply be. With each breath, you relax even more deeply."

"Allow this bubble to carry you further, beyond space and time, until there is nothing around you but your own presence. Here, in the timeless now, in the ever-present future, there is nothing to do, nothing to think about. Just be. Your mind expands, and your consciousness opens wide, as the waves of existence unfold like pages in a book. The path of your soul lies before you. Are you ready to explore its depths?"

In my mind, I answer yes. A soft white light floods my vision, and as it fills my mind's eye, I slip fully into a hypnotic state.

Catherine's voice remains gentle. "You've now begun to leave the Earth's astral plane and are traveling deeper into the spirit world. I want you to tell me what you feel."

"I feel silence … it's so peaceful …" I reply softly.

"Is anyone coming to meet you?"

"Yes … it's my mom. But it's not my mom … it's a soul named Ophelia. She is always here when I cross over. When I am no longer on Earth."

"Has Ophelia been with you in other lifetimes, or does she stay behind in the spirit world?"

"No, she is with me often. I need her."

"Can you describe what Ophelia's soul looks like to you right now?"

"A youngish woman … as I remember her best … strikingly beautiful with delicate features … a nurturing look in her eyes … so much charisma."

"And what do you feel when you look at her?"

"A deep tranquility … energy … love. When I meet her gaze, I see light. A connection so real, undeniable."

"Could she be your spirit guide? Welcoming you back to the spirit world after each lifetime?"

I shake my head slowly, emotion swelling inside me. "Maybe … yes. I think so." Tears spill down my cheeks, unbidden, as the weight of this truth sinks in. "Ophelia is, indeed, my mom."

"What are you and Ophelia doing right now in the spirit world?"

"She's taken me to a kind of reunion. I see my family and my friends from many lifetimes. There's no judgment in the spirit world, no need for approval—only peace."

"It sounds like judgment —and seeking validation—is something you struggle with in human life."

"Yes, it's deep within me—this need to please. It's attached to me like a weight I've carried for centuries."

"Let's allow your consciousness to drift further back in time. With each breath, let yourself travel to a lifetime that holds significance for you. What do you see? Where does your soul take you?"

I shift slightly on the sofa, still enveloped in the deep pull of hypnosis. My mind feels clear and fluid as if every thought glides effortlessly through the space around me. My body is weightless, completely relaxed, like a leaf floating on still water.

Catherine's voice is gentle, almost a whisper. "Back in the bubble, you continue to float … float … drift effortlessly, guided to where you need to be. Take a deep breath and feel yourself settle. Where are you now, Reilly?"

CHAPTER 18
phillip and marie

My memory anchors in the post-World War II era. I hear a gentle chime echoing through the space, surrounded by about 50 other people seated close together. A cheerful woman's voice comes over the intercom: "Ladies and gentlemen, we'll be landing soon. Please have your trash ready as I come around to collect it." Shit ... I'm on an airplane.

The body I'm in feels different. But it's still me—it's my same soul. I touch my face—I have a mustache and bushy eyebrows, and I'm wearing a fedora. I'm a man in this lifetime, and I presume I'm living in the late 1940s by the way I'm dressed. Pulling my plane ticket from my book on the tray table, I see the name Phillip Jenson. I'm on my way to Chicago from NYC.

As I slide the ticket back into the crevice of the book, a photograph slips free and flutters onto my lap. It's of a young woman in her 20s, her short, curly hair framing a face lit up by a bright-eyed smile. She's standing in front of the Ferris wheel at Chicago's Navy Pier. There's something familiar in her gaze. I turn the photo over and read the words scrawled on the back: "The one that got away. My dearest Maryanne." A wave of recognition runs through me. Those eyes—full of life and longing—I know them. It's undeniable. Maryanne is someone very familiar, but it's still too hazy to piece together.

A heavy, sinking feeling spreads through me as this memory comes into focus. I'm on this airplane for two reasons: to find a new career path in journalism—after being unceremoniously fired from The New York Post—and to track down Maryanne. The first goal feels daunting like a door slammed shut on years of work and ambition. But the second ... that's something different, something personal, a loose thread I can't leave hanging. The stewardess approaches, her smile unwavering as she takes the two empty glasses of brandy from my tray.

Just then, a weird twinge pierces through my body.

Without warning, the plane lurches into a sudden, sharp dive, the cabin tilting as passengers are thrown against their seats. For what feels like an eternity, the aircraft spirals before leveling out, but only briefly. Screams fill the air—women clutch their husbands tightly, their faces pale with terror. The cabin trembles violently, and a thick, acrid scent of smoke begins to creep through the air. The stewardess, her voice strained with fear, yells for everyone to fasten their seatbelts. Then, the plane drops again, more violently this time.

I glance around and a grim certainty settles over me—this is the end for all of us. There's no escape. Everything feels surreal as if I'm watching from behind a veil, detached from the panic around me. My mind races, but my body is paralyzed, too stunned even to scream. My hands grip the armrests, numb yet steady, and somehow I'm still clutching the photograph of Maryanne.

I turn to the window, watching the ground rush up to meet us, faster and faster. In my mind, I whisper: Maryanne, you'll always be with me.

As I watch my past life play out before me, I fully remember Phillip's life—always chasing something or someone, always believing there was more time. And now, it's all slipping away. No more chances, no more moments. It's just ... an end.

I gasp sharply in Catherine's office, my breath coming in uneven, frantic waves. My chest rises and falls as I struggle to steady myself, the remnants of that vivid vision clinging to me. Catherine's soothing voice cuts through the chaos, grounding me. Her words are gentle yet firm, pulling me back to the stillness of the moment. I remain rooted in the hypnotic state, my mind teetering on the edge of consciousness. Without hesitation, she urges me onward, guiding me deeper into the unknown, and encouraging me to unlock yet another lifetime.

"You're back in the protective bubble, Reilly, gently floating … allowing yourself to drift, this time landing softly in another lifetime."

A gray alley cat darts past me, its fur slick with rain, as I crouch near a puddle—hoping it's nothing more than rainwater or runoff from the crumbling buildings above. The cold bites through my thin clothes and each gust of wind cuts like a knife as it howls through the narrow space between two dilapidated buildings. It's the 1870s in Paris, but time feels irrelevant in this forgotten corner of the city. Everything I own is on me: the threadbare clothes clinging to my shivering body, a satchel with my paints and a few canvases, and three bottles of absinthe—each already three-fourths empty, their hollow promises lingering like ghosts.

I stumble to my feet, unsteady and drunk—again. A starving artist, they call me, though the truth is darker. I take payment in drugs, or sex— anything to numb the constant ache. Tonight, though, I'm alone, and the silence churns up old wounds: abandonment, rejection, the disapproval that's always gnawed at me since my family cast me out.

My mère forced me out of our flat when I was 18 after rumors spread that I had same-sex desires for my artist friend at university. It was true, though I denied it with every fiber of my being. But none of it mattered. I was tossed out like a piece of trash, discarded and unloved for who I am. Now, at 22, I'm lost—adrift in a life that seems to get no better with time.

There's one woman, though, who has always seen me for who I truly am—Miss Juliette. In her 40s, she's a wise woman. Never married. Always a socialite. I met her at a writer's literary circle, and the moment she learned

I was an artist, we felt an instant connection. She commissioned me to paint her dog, Gaston, and from that moment on, we deeply bonded. She offers me a place to sleep on unbearably cold nights and acts like a motherly figure to me.

Most importantly, she treats me with dignity. She respects who I am. But it's been a while since I've seen Miss Juliette—too long, really. I went off on my own, to experience life. I needed to grow up, to carve my own path, but instead, I fell into the deep shadows of this city, losing myself in drugs, in poverty, in my own despair. And now, all I want is to find my way back to her. Maybe she'll take me in, at least for tonight. Maybe, if I'm lucky, she'll see past my mistakes and offer me a future, a place to stay where I can rebuild myself.

I arrive at her apartment just as I remembered it—grand yet unpretentious, tucked away on a quiet street lined with cobblestones. The building's exterior, weathered by time, bores the elegance of Haussmann's renovations, with tall windows framed by wrought-iron balconies. As I climb to her third-floor residence, something feels different, smells different—the ambiance of the once light and airy corridors now feels dark and drab. I knock on the door. No answer. I continue knocking several more times.

A door creaks open across the hall, and an elderly resident steps out. "Who are you looking for, miss?" he asks, his voice kind but cautious.

"Oh, um … I'm looking for Miss Juliette," I reply, hopeful.

The man's face falls. "Oh dear," he murmurs, shaking his head. "Miss Juliette is gone. She passed away … about a year ago."

"What?" The word tears out of me, sharp and disbelieving. "How?"

He sighs, eyes cast downward. "She drowned, poor thing. It was an accident. She was out on the Seine with some friends for the afternoon. Slipped underneath the water and … they couldn't save her."

I stand frozen, my chest tightening. "My God," I whisper, the weight of the words sinking in, shattering me from the inside out. I walk back onto the streets of Paris in a state of shock.

Completely devastated, it feels as if all the good in the world has been stripped away. With trembling hands, I reach into my satchel and swallow the last bitter sips of absinthe, its warmth doing little to dull the hollow ache inside me. Miss Juliette was the closest thing I had to a motherly figure and now she's gone—another piece of me taken, leaving nothing but emptiness. Hope, once flickering dimly, now slips away like sand through my fingers. Numb, I begin to walk, my feet moving without thought, my mind locked in a haze. My vision narrows, everything blurring except the path ahead. It leads me to the Pont des Arts, the bridge of lovers, adorned with thousands of locks.

The river swirls violently beneath me, its dark waters churning like a storm. It looks so cold, so unforgiving as if it's waiting to swallow me whole. I feel like I have no other choice—nothing left to hold on to. The world feels like it's closing in, leaving no room for escape.

This river is where Miss Juliette died. It feels almost fitting, as if by jumping here, I'll be with her again—where she last was. I trusted her in a way I've never trusted anyone else. Maybe this is about returning to the only person who ever saw me, whoever cared enough to see past all my broken pieces. My hands tremble as I grip the railing, every muscle in my body shaking. With one last breath, I hoist myself up onto the edge, the wind biting against my skin. And I let go.

Startled, I gasp for breath, my heart racing. Catherine's soothing voice cuts through the panic, grounding me with simple instructions yet again. "Feel the sofa beneath you, Reilly," she says gently. "Notice the texture of your clothes against your skin, and the steady rise and fall of your chest as you breathe."

Calming down, Catherine continues, "We're almost ready to return to the present, but before we do, is there anything specific you're yearning to understand from your time in the spirit world?"

"Yes," I say emphatically. "What's the meaning of 806?"

In a gentle shimmer, Ophelia reappears, smiling. "I'm glad you're tuned in to this. Repeatedly seeing the same number is known as an "angel number"—a sign from the universe. These numbers carry unique vibrations and serve as a reassuring message that your life is on the right path, aligning with your true essence. It's a reminder to trust the journey you're on."

"Fascinating. All this time, I thought this number was haunting me. Knowing it's actually a positive sign is such a relief," I say, feeling a newfound sense of calm.

Catherine's gentle voice rises. We're going to start coming back to the present, Reilly. Take a deep breath in … and slowly exhale. In a moment, I'll count up from one to five. Each breath will pull you further from the intensity of your visions, gaining clarity with every inhale.

One … begin to bring awareness to your hands and feet. Two … feel the energy returning to your body, gently waking up. Three … becoming more conscious, and more aware of the room around you. Four … feeling clear, centered, and ready to return. Five … when you're ready, open your eyes, feeling refreshed, relaxed, and fully present."

I open my eyes wide, slowly taking in the space around me as my vision adjusts to the gentle glow of the fluorescent lights in Catherine's office. "Wow … that was incredible. I'm honestly speechless," I say, my words soft and measured.

"You did a marvelous job, Reilly," Catherine responds, her voice filled with encouragement. "You allowed yourself to journey through glimpses of your past lives, uncovering insights that I hope resonate with your present. I trust you'll find some answers to some deeper questions about your existence, purpose, and path ahead."

After finishing the checkout process, I step out onto the bustling streets of New York City. Manhattan is alive with energy—tourist-filled buses rumble by, taxis weave through traffic, and street performers captivate on every corner. It's such a sharp contrast to where I was moments ago. My mind races with thoughts of Phillip and Marie, trying to piece together everything I've just seen and felt.

Phillip—a failed writer, endlessly chasing a woman, consumed by heartache, lost in a plane crash. Marie—cast out by her own family, a starving artist drowning in drink, falling in love with an older woman before dying by her own hand. And then, of course, Ophelia which is, in fact, Mom—the astonishing realization that she's my spirit guide, there to greet me each time I return to the spirit realm after every lifetime.

I taxi over to the pier to meet Alexis for our kayaking adventure. She's already arranged everything—two kayaks, paddles, and life jackets. "It's on me, birthday girl," she says with a playful wink. The morning rain has given way to clear skies, and the bright glow of the sun highlights her black hair and porcelain skin. With a smile, she hands me a small gift, which I eagerly unwrap. Inside is a delicate necklace with a lotus charm.

"The lotus symbolizes transformation," Alexis explains warmly, "and it can be a daily reminder of the incredible journey you've been on and the inner work you've done." Her words fill me with a deep appreciation as I hold the charm, feeling its energy between us. I immediately put it on—the cool metal resting against my skin.

As we paddle down the majestic Hudson River, gliding past other kayakers and the occasional boat, Alexis leans in, her eyes bright with curiosity. She's eager to hear the details of my session with the past life regression hypnotherapist, and I'm equally thrilled to share it all. The river's gentle current mirrors my mind's unusual calmness as I try to put my experience into words, the excitement bubbling up with each stroke of the paddle.

"Before I surprise you with actual memories of my past lives," I say, a spark of mystery in my voice, "can I share my learned philosophy about human existence and the beyond?" Vibrance is practically radiating from me.

"Reilly, yes, tell me," Alexis answers, her curiosity intense.

"Okay … well … we've all lived 100s … even 1000s of lifetimes. Reincarnation is real. Our human bodies are merely vessels for our souls, temporary homes for our souls between life on Earth and the afterlife in the spirit realm. Death isn't the end—ever. When we leave this world, our souls journey to the spirit realm—a heavenly, expansive place where we're greeted by our personal spirit guides." I pause, making sure Alexis is following.

"Okay, Reilly. I'm tracking," she says, her voice filled with wonder.

"Every soul belongs to a "soul family"—a group of about 10 to 15 souls that hold special significance across each lifetime. Before each new life, you work closely with your spirit guide to plan out your next lifetime on Earth, from choosing your parents to setting up key challenges, even deciding on your eventual death experience. The purpose of each lifetime is to help your soul evolve, release bad karma, and learn lessons. Earth is essentially a school for souls."

My excitement is contagious as I continue, "And here's the amazing part—everything is connected! There's a reason behind everything. While we have free will, the major people we meet and big life choices we make are carefully mapped out before we ever arrive here on Earth. The purpose of life on Earth is to become the best versions of ourselves."Alexis stares at me, her eyes wide with awe, as if a whole new world has just opened up before her. "Wow … Reilly, this is … really mind-blowing," she says, her voice soft with amazement. I sense some hesitation in her voice.

"The idea that everything—every person, every experience—happens for a reason … it changes everything." She pauses, her gaze distant as if she's piecing together her own experiences in light of what I've told her. "I feel … enlightened, I think. I wonder what that means about us?"

Chapter 19
connect the dots

As I push through the heavy doors of Tattoo NYC, a laidback joint tucked away in the heart of my West Village neighborhood, I feel an instant rush of cool air against my skin—a blessed escape from the blistering July heat outside. It's been a month since I closed the chapter on my one year of no dating, and I've had that full month to process 365 days of becoming a truer, more enlightened version of myself.

Choosing to get a second tattoo was an easy decision. People say tattoos are like potato chips … you can never have just one. My biggest life lesson—"Trust the Journey"—will soon be etched into my skin, a lasting reminder of a belief I now hold close: this life, with all its unpredictability, unfolds exactly as it should.

A tall, solidly built guy steps out from behind a heavy black curtain, his frame filling the space. He's got a fedora perched on his head, a blue tank stretched taut over his chest, and tattoos snaking up both arms to his knuckles. "Welcome in. Are you here for an appointment?" he asks in a surprisingly soft, gentle tone.

"Yes, I am," I say, feeling the cool air inside settle over me. "I have an appointment with Gretchen. I might be a bit early."

"I'll let her know you're here. Feel free to look around or take a seat," he says casually, as he organizes a stack of receipts on the front desk. "I'm Frankie, by the way."

"Nice to meet you," I reply, matching his tone—before turning to a nearby wall covered with tattoo designs and photos of past patrons proudly showing off their new ink.

My phone buzzes—a text from Quinn. She's up north this weekend at Wildwood State Park, camping with Connor and Anna. I'm happy she's spending time in the outdoors for a change. Lately, she's been pouring herself into acting and modeling, and from the sound of it, she's really thriving. Basketball feels like a distant memory now, a part of our lives that's faded away as Quinn steps into this new chapter with a spark I haven't seen in her before.

(2:11 pm) Quinn:

Hey Mom. I just wanted to say I love you. You are the best! Send a photo of your new tattoo 😘

My eyes well up with tears. Out of nowhere, Quinn's message touches something deep within me—it means everything. With a smile and a lump in my throat, I text her back.

(2:13 pm) Reilly:

I love you, too, Quinny-girl. I am so lucky to be your mom. I'm at the tattoo parlor now! ❤️

Walking toward me from the back of the shop, Gretchen appears—dressed head to toe in black with a backward cap, exuding an effortless, cool energy. Her petite figure and long brown hair catches my attention. She sports pink sparkly lipstick, a variety of piercings, and an unmistakable vibe that's both confident and queer. She looks to be around my age, maybe a bit younger, with an easy swagger that instantly makes me feel like I'm in good hands.

She greets me with a friendly smirk and an easy welcoming, "Hey there, you must be Reilly. I'm Gretchen. Nice to meet you.""Hey, Gretchen. Nice to meet you, too," I say, wondering if she has picked up on my queerness, too. I'm in my ripped skinny jeans, classic white tank, white sneakers, and, of course, my signature backward trucker hat. As we make small talk, I follow her to the back of the shop, where her tattoo chair waits, the buzz of needles in the background adding a thrill to the moment.

"So … "Trust the Journey," huh?" Gretchen asks with an intriguing look like she's itching to know the whole backstory. "I love it. I'm guessing there's a pretty amazing story behind this one, right?"

I chuckle, feeling a mix of excitement and vulnerability. "Yeah, you could say that," I reply, my voice steady. "Life has a way of throwing us around, and every twist and turn—whether it's painful or joyful—feels like part of a bigger plan. This tattoo isn't just ink for me; it's a promise to live with openness, to embrace the unknown, and to trust that every step—even the shaky ones—is carrying me forward."

Gretchen's eyes soften as she listens, and nods slowly, almost as if my words hit close to home. "I get that. I've got a couple of tattoos myself that keep me grounded, especially when life feels like it's all over the place. There's just something about carrying those reminders with you, you know?" She gestures to a small compass tattoo on her wrist. "This one's my own little reminder to stay even-keeled, even when everything else is spinning. It's like wearing a piece of yourself you can hold onto."

She gets it. As I settle into Gretchen's chair, a calm washes over me. I watch her lay the stencil carefully on my forearm, aligning it with precision. "You ready?" she asks, her eyes meeting mine with a reassuring warmth.

"Yes, I'm more than ready," I reply, excitedly—noticing her gaze lingers a little longer into my eyes.

Gretchen prepares her workspace and insists I start telling her about my story and what's led me to this point. I can see she's insightful and has a gentle heart beneath her rough-looking exterior.

But where do I begin?

I give Gretchen the quick rundown of my year—the dating hiatus, the deep self-reflection, the journey toward self-love, and my understanding of life, death, and the afterlife. Clearing my throat, I add, "This year has been incredible, honestly. Now that I've had some time to step back and reflect on it, I can finally connect the dots. I see how the challenges and events in my current life have shaped me and brought me closer to understanding my true self."

Gretchen leans in, her eyes wide with curiosity. "And tell me about connecting the dots. What have you learned?"

I take a deep breath, feeling the question wash over me. "To trust the journey," I reply, with a calm, steady certainty that feels true to my core.

"Hence the tattoo," we both say in unison.

Gretchen pauses, giving me a thoughtful, kind stare. "Wow, that's … that's really something."

As she begins inking my tattoo, the needle's sharp buzz fills the air. The first sting jolts through my arm, intense and electric, but I breathe into it, letting my body adjust. Gradually, the initial shock fades, and a strange calm settles in—a rhythm between pain and acceptance, like the words I'm choosing to wear.

"So, for real, tell me about some of these dots you've connected," Gretchen says, her tone sincere.

I nod, feeling ready to share. Gretchen already feels like a safe zone. "Alright," I begin, the words flowing naturally. "Phillip and Marie were both alcoholics, just as I am in this lifetime—though now I'm a recovering one. Across lifetimes, I've learned that alcohol has been a haunting presence, an unshakable force shaping my choices and trapping me in cycles of struggle and surrender. I've tried and failed so many times to break free, caught in the same painful loop … until this lifetime," I pause, a quiet pride swelling in my chest. "191 days sober. I think I've finally learned the lesson I've been challenged with each time on Earth. I'm determined to break the cycle of alcoholism—for myself, for my daughter, Quinn, and for whatever lifetimes may follow."

I continue cautiously, as Gretchen works on my tattoo, focused, her hand moving with practiced precision.

"Here's another one. I've always carried this label of shy," I say with a soft laugh, realizing how differently I see it now. "It used to hold me back, affecting my confidence. When my mom introduced me as "terribly shy," I think she meant it endearingly. And when I was voted "Shyest Girl" in high school, I can almost see it as a compliment now—850 students knew who I was, after all. It's clear now: I'm not actually shy. I'm an introvert, a *noticer*. A thinker, an observer. I treasure my solitude. I don't care for small talk; I value real, meaningful connections. I'm reserved—until I'm not. If we connect, you matter to me." I pause, smiling. "Just last December, I went to Tokyo alone, met wonderful strangers, and came back renewed, refreshed. Not once did anyone label me as shy."

Gretchen listens intently, nodding along while I open up the details of my life to her.

"Next up: approval-seeking. I have been the ultimate approval-seeker, but I've finally cracked the code on this exhausting, misguided habit. A few examples: 1.) For three decades, I hid my true self, terrified that coming out gay would devastate my parents. 2.) Growing up with a disabled sibling, I took on the role of the happy, carefree child everyone expected, but inside, I was a deeply anxious kid with a skewed view of the world. 3.) I married my best friend—a man I was never attracted to—and pretended to be for 16 years. 4.) Later, I stayed far too long in a toxic situationship, afraid of disappointing the other person." I pause, feeling the weight of my own words lift. "I've made peace with people-pleasing. And I've learned. I've learned to say no, to honor myself, to put my own needs first—to love myself. That's the journey I'm carrying forward now."

"Your story is fascinating," Gretchen says, looking up for a moment to lock eyes. "I didn't come out of the closet until I was 28, either. I'm 33 now." She gives a small, understanding smile. "I can relate to being a people-pleaser—always bending over backward, never wanting to let anyone down or make waves. It took me a long time to realize that I was shrinking myself just to keep others comfortable." She resumes her work, the needle buzzing back to life. "Hearing your story, though … it's inspiring. Makes me think of all the ways I still need to trust my own journey, too. Keep going, I love hearing this."

"Okay, if you say so," I reply with a playful laugh. "This past year, my dream of becoming a novelist has been truly ignited. In past lives, as Phillip, I was a journalist for the *New York Post*, and as Marie, I was an artist, pouring my thoughts into intricate paintings. In this lifetime, my love is for creative writing—bringing stories to life, and creating worlds for readers to explore. As an introvert, I've discovered I'm far more comfortable expressing myself on the page than in conversation. From Mr. Langston's seventh-grade creative writing class to spilling my heart in a letter to my ex-husband, asking for a divorce, writing has always been my truest voice. Becoming a novelist is a calling I can't shake."

"What do you do for a living now?" Gretchen asks, her curiosity evident.

"I'm in PR," I reply flatly. "But honestly, I'm thinking about quitting. Seriously."

Her face lights up. "That's so bold of you. I wish I could quit my job and go after my passion, too," she says, a bit wistfully.

I tilt my head, intrigued. "What's your passion?"

"I'm all about animals," she says, a spark of pride in her eyes. "I'd love to open an adoption center for cats and dogs right here in the West Village. Right now, I'm fostering 10 cats in my apartment, and I've got two more coming in on Monday!"

"Wow, that's incredible!" I say, genuinely impressed. "What an amazing purpose to have."

"Thank you. Now carry on with more insights you've learned about your life from this past year. I'm getting more and more inspired to do my own year of no dating and self-discovery," Gretchen says.

"Oh my God, this next one's a doozy," I say, bracing myself.

"Ooooh, do tell," Gretchen replies, sitting up straighter as she refills her tattoo machine, clearly engaged.

I chuckle, feeling a bit awkward. "Alright, well … so … I have a domination/submission fetish. Probably TMI for someone I just met."

"Girl, no judgment here," Gretchen says with a grin, completely unfazed. "I used to be in adult films."

"Alright, well … I have this Mommy/Babygirl fantasy," I begin, measuring each word. "It probably stems from my complicated history with mother figures. There's Marie, who was kicked out for being gay, and then there's my own struggle to connect with my mom in this lifetime before watching her pass away. Marie found love with Miss Juliette, an older woman who made her feel safe and protected. And maybe I'm chasing something similar. Recently, I spent 24 hours with a woman named Mistress MacKenzie, a dominatrix who took on the "Mommy" role for me. It was incredible. For the first time, I felt confident, sexy, and powerful—from simply … letting go. It was trust, feeling safe enough to be vulnerable. Allowing myself to be nurtured. That night with Mistress MacKenzie unlocked something deep within me, almost like our energies had met before, guiding me closer to who I am."

I pause, taking a breath. "I've learned that my mother is my spirit guide each time I leave Earth and return to the spirit realm. I remember her soul as it was before life's challenges took over … before her focus had to shift. As a young child, she was still able to pour her love into me, to nurture and care for me before my sister was born. I ache for that version of her—the mother I lost emotionally as a child and physically as an adult. And somehow, being cared for by a maternal figure now fills a deep void within me, answering a longing to be seen, loved, and truly cared for."

"Wow, that is so deep and reflective," Gretchen says admiringly. "I'm nearly finished with your tattoo, but got any more stories?"

"Okay, so … there's this girl …" I begin, feeling a little hesitant.

"Aha, there's always a girl," Gretchen says with a knowing wink.

"Remember how I mentioned I stayed stuck in a situationship for way too long?" I continue, glancing down. "Well … Alexis. She always resurfacing in my life, like some kind of unfinished chapter I can't close."

Gretchen nods, a look of understanding in her eyes. "It sounds like she's a huge part of your life—almost like a ghost that keeps lingering, something you're drawn to but can't quite let go of."

"Yes, exactly," I say, feeling a knot of both fear and certainty tightening in my chest. "In my past life vision as Phillip, I carried around this photograph of a woman named Maryanne, someone he was yearning for—planning to find in Chicago before his fatal plane crash. The woman in the photo looked strangely familiar, but I couldn't quite place her at the time. Now I know who it was. Maryanne is Alexis, here in the present."

"Oh my God, are you sure?" Gretchen asks, her eyes wide with surprise.

I nod, holding her gaze, my voice certain. "Yes. It was Maryanne's eyes—the way they sparkled, just like Alexis's. You can always recognize a soul through their eyes. I know, without a doubt, that Alexis is someone I've been chasing across lifetimes. But, we always seem to be out of sync."

Gretchen leans forward, her face thoughtful. "Maybe she's a twin flame. Someone who's like a mirror to your soul—someone who makes you confront everything you need to, even if it's messy or painful.""Wow, I've never considered that possibility," I reply.

"What is a soulmate to you?" Gretchen asks without hesitation.

"Soulmates come into our lives to teach us something or help us grow. Sometimes, they're only around for a short time, and sometimes, they're with us forever. But the connection is intense, like meeting a part of ourselves we didn't know was missing."

I glance at Gretchen, who's listening intently, and continue. "It's this feeling of recognition, like looking into someone's eyes and seeing pieces of our own story. And it doesn't have to be romantic or even lifelong. It's just … two souls that keep finding each other, always bringing something important to the other."

Gretchen's eyes glisten, teetering on the edge of tears, but I can tell she's holding them back. She straightens her posture and glances toward the front of the shop, as if to gather herself, hiding the emotion in her gaze. After a steadying breath, she says softly, "I'm finished here. So … what do you think of your new tattoo?"

I look down, feeling a deep sense of pride and alignment as if my core philosophy is now woven into the very fabric of who I am. "It's perfect."

As I make my way to the front of the shop to snap my showcase photo and settle up, a realization hits me—I don't want this connection with Gretchen to end here. I turn to her, feeling a rare kind of gratitude. "Thanks for letting me share my life with you," I say earnestly. "It's not every day that someone really listens."

She raises an eyebrow, her response blunt and immediate. "Are you kidding? I loved hearing it. Fascinating. Honestly, your story makes me want to start my own journey of becoming."

"A bit of advice … go into it without a plan. No structure, no anticipations, no attaching to outcomes. Just fly-by-the-seat of your pants and see where your journey takes you," I recommend.

"Okay, thanks for the guidance," Gretchen indicates.

I pause, nerves flickering beneath my confidence. "Can we hang out sometime?"

"Absolutely." She writes her cell phone number on the back of her business card. "But do me a favor—leave that Alexis chick out of it," she says with a playful smirk.

CHAPTER 20
snow cones

Quinn leaps out of the car, clutching her script, her eyes bright with excitement. She's so eager she barely remembers to say goodbye. Today's a big day—she's been handpicked to audition for a Super Bowl commercial for PepsiCo. All the late nights, all the hustle—it's finally paying off.

"Go get 'em, Quinn!" I shout out the passenger side window, grinning as I watch her stride toward the building with purpose. "Call me when you're done, and I'll be here to pick you up!"

A whole other year has passed.

Life's happened. Things have changed. Time moves on.

I'm still riding the wave of self-exploration and enlightenment, and I have no intention of stepping off. I'm not ready to close that door—in fact, I hope to leave it open. As human beings, we're here to constantly evolve. That doesn't stop after one meaningful, transformative year.

I pull into a parking garage nearby and wander toward a charming little tavern on the corner—perfect for a cool escape from this, once again, sweltering summer heat. Inside, the air is still, a reprieve from the bustling world outside, and I sink into a cozy booth. I open the drink menu, eyes trailing over the icy cocktails and fine wines.

A waiter strolls up, his tone easy. "What can I get you to drink? Mai Tais are half off until 5 o'clock."

"I'll have an unsweetened iced tea, please—and nachos," I say, catching the subtle shift in his expression as he mentally downgrades me to a low-spender.

But today, that doesn't bother me. I'm 566 days sober—a milestone that once felt impossible, is now a point of pride. I can sit here, unmoved by the parade of drinks that pass by. These days, I walk through the liquor aisle at the grocery store like it's any other section. Unfazed. Free.

I pull out my laptop, lifting the lid to a blank email, save for a single line blinking back at me. My fingers hover over the keyboard, poised to continue, but my gaze lingers on the words already typed:

Dear Alexis …

A sudden burst of laughter jolts me, and I glance up. A group of businessmen, loud and boisterous, stumbles into the restaurant, claiming a cluster of seats at the bar. The air fills with their booming voices and the clink of glassware, pulling my attention from the screen. Just like that, the serene moment I'd carved out slips away.

Sitting here on a Friday afternoon, I'm reminded how weekdays have taken on a whole new rhythm. No longer bound to an office, to mind-numbing meetings, or the relentless ping of emails, I've found freedom in these calm, unhurried hours. Six months ago, I walked away from the corporate grind and poured myself into something that feels real. I'm a writer now. It has become my foundation, my greatest calling, and somehow, *Unapologetically Herself*—my first novel—has found its way into readers' hands. Making its way to the *New York Times* bestsellers list, a sequel now waits, the story slowly unfolding each day. Next month, I'll start creative writing classes at The New School—a career step I'm proud to embrace.

The waiter stops by to set down my iced tea just as my phone buzzes. It's Connor. I swipe to answer. "Hey, what's up?"

"Hey! How's Quinn doing? Is she in the audition?" he asks, his voice cheerful and easygoing.

"Yeah, she's in there now. She was so excited going in—I can't wait to see how she feels when she comes out," I say, smiling. "So ... how are the newlyweds?"

Connor chuckles. "We're good. Settling into the new place, but, man, unpacking is a bitch. But hey, uh ... I didn't just call to check on the audition."

"Oh?" I reply, a hint of eagerness slipping into my voice.

"Yeah. So ... Anna and I have been talking, and we were wondering if you and Quinn might want to join us on a Caribbean cruise over Christmas. Kind of ... a family trip?"

My eyes widen. "Wait—are you serious?"

"Yeah, Reilly, I'm serious," he says, a little softer this time. "Look, it doesn't have to be awkward between us. More than anything, I'm thinking about Quinn. Imagine how much fun she'd have if we were all there together."

I pause, feeling a swell of hope rise within me. Could this really be the beginning of the blended family I've dreamed of since the divorce? "Yeah, okay! I'll confirm with Quinn but I'm confident it's a yes," I say, my voice voice alight with enthusiasm. "Just let me know the booking details when you have them."

As I hang up, a gentle thrill runs through me—maybe, just maybe, this is a new chapter for all of us.

Settling back into the booth, I take a slow, steadying breath, savoring the crunch and salt of a few nachos before turning my focus back to the laptop.

Dear Alexis ...

But before I can type another word, my phone's alarm chimes—1:15 pm, right on schedule. My daily reminder to call Raegan. A few months ago, I got her a cellphone, a small gesture to strengthen our connection. Now, each day at this time, I call her, creating a pattern, a sweet ritual just for us. She knows she can reach out any time, but this call is our anchor, a moment where we don't let life get in the way.

Hi, Reilly!" Raegan answers, her voice bright with excitement. "How are you?"

"Hi, Raegan!" I reply, smiling at her energy. "I'm good! Just sitting at a restaurant, waiting for Quinn to finish her audition." I know she may not fully understand, but I like sharing these little details with her.

"Oh, that sounds nice. I'm playing with Ninja and working on my puzzle," she says proudly.

"That sounds like a pretty great day, Raegan. How's Dad doing?" I ask, shifting the conversation gently.

"He's … sleeping on the couch," she says, her voice softening a bit, tinged with disappointment.

"Well, hey," I say, lifting my tone, "do you remember what's happening tomorrow?"

"You're coming over to visit!" she chirps, a spark returning to her voice.

"That's right! And who am I bringing with me?" I ask, hoping she remembers.

"Quinny?" she ventures, a little uncertain.

"Not quite," I tease, giving her a hint. "It's your favorite person …"

"Gretchen!" she exclaims, her excitement bubbling over.

"Yes, you got it! We'll see you tomorrow around noon. Love you, Raegan."

"Love you too, Reilly!" she says, and I can hear her happiness as we end the call.

As I shift my focus back to my email to Alexis for the third time, my mind drifts to that day last year—almost exactly at this hour—when I met Gretchen at the tattoo parlor and ended up spilling my life story to her. She listened with such compassion, without any hint of judgment, and our connection felt effortless as if it had always been there, waiting for us to find it.

Inspired by my own dating sabbatical, Gretchen embarked on her own journey of no dating for a year and radical self-discovery. Fast friends jiving on the same frequency, we spent countless hours meeting at coffee shops philosophizing about life, volunteering together at animal shelters, and joining me on the long drives to Dad's and Raegan's for extra company.

My focus returns and I stare back at my email to Alexis.

Dear Alexis,

How's London treating you? Are you causing any trouble over there? Just kidding. :)

I miss you. The other day, I walked past Patsy's Pizzeria, and it stopped me in my tracks. I could smell the pizza from down the block, and all I could think about was our spot. It made me smile.

I just wanted to say how grateful I am that we gave our relationship another chance this year. We chose to invest in each other and rebuild, and while it came with its challenges, the joy and love we rediscovered made it deeply fulfilling and something I'll always cherish.

When you left for Europe last month, it felt so sudden. Were you running toward something—or maybe away from something?

Whatever the reason, I know one thing for sure: you're meant to be in my life. Even though things didn't work out between us romantically, that doesn't mean our story ends—it continues, stretching beyond time and distance.

Let me know how you're doing. I'd love to hear from you.

Love,
Reilly

A wave of peace washes over me as I hit send, as if the weight of the unspoken has finally lifted. My hand instinctively reaches for the lotus necklace Alexis gave me for my birthday last year—a small token of comfort—but my fingers meet only bare skin. Panic flickers to life as I pat my clothes and scan the space around me, hoping to find it. When the realization sets in that it must have broken and fallen off somewhere along the way, a strange stillness takes its place. Maybe it's not just a loss, but a quiet message from the universe—a reminder to embrace what lies ahead without holding on too tightly to what was.

Just then, my phone buzzes—it's Quinn. Her audition is over.

At the apartment, hours later, Quinn is buzzing with excitement, replaying every moment of her audition. Trying to keep her grounded, I suggest we take a walk to Polar Paradise—something to cool our minds and soak in the eventful day.

Sitting at a picnic table outside of the shop, we savor our Watermelon Wave and Cotton Candy Cloud snow cones. The summer night is alive with the hum of the West Village—distant car horns, bursts of laughter from nearby diners, and the rhythmic clatter of heels on pavement. Neon signs cast a soft, colorful glow on the sidewalk, and the warm air carries the mingling scents of asphalt, street food, and traces of someone's cologne. I can't help but bask in the pure joy of this occasion, even as I realize my Quinny-girl is growing up far too quickly for my heart to keep up. The preteen sass is starting to surface these days, and pretty soon she won't want to get snow cones with me anymore.

"I love you, Quinny-girl," I say, my voice quiet but full of meaning.

"Love you, too, Mom," Quinn replies with a sweet smile, sticky hands holding her cone.

As we finish, I lean in with a playful smirk. "When you go to Dad's tomorrow morning, ask him about his plans for Christmas. You'll like what he has to say."

Quinn tilts her head, curiosity lighting up her face, but I leave her guessing. Some surprises are worth waiting for.

"Look, Mom! Those are a few friends from school! Can I go say hi?" Quinn asks, her mood boosted with energy.

"Absolutely, go say hi. Have fun," I reply, watching her dart off.

Before I can dwell too much on this bittersweet point in time, I hear my name, spoken softly from behind.

"Reilly, hey."

I turn around and see Gretchen, standing there with a beaming smile.

"Oh, hey! What are you doing here?" I say surprised.

"I had a feeling you'd be here tonight," she says, her smile growing bigger. "Quinn's big audition, a warm summer evening … it just made sense that you two would end up at your favorite spot for a treat."

Her words carry a knowing warmth, and I can't help but gleam. Gretchen knows me—it's like we're on the same wavelength.

This past year, we have built an incredible bond. What began as a chance encounter in that tattoo parlor has blossomed into a deep connection rooted in our shared commitment to growth, healing, and self-discovery.

"Can I join you for a bit? I see Quinn over there with her friends," Gretchen asks, her voice tinged with sympathy as she gestures toward the nearby group.

"Of course," I say, sliding over to make room. "Want a snow cone? My treat."

She smiles warmly. "No, thank you. I just downed a Starbucks Caramel Macchiato, so I think I've hit my sugar quota for the day."

I chuckle softly, then pause, letting the moment settle. Finally, I draw in a deep breath. "I emailed Alexis today," I say, my tone calm but deliberate. "And I just want to say thank you, Gretchen. For being the friend I didn't even know I needed this past year. For sticking by me through all the ups and downs of my ridiculously messy relationship with Alexis. I have closure now."

"Anything for you, Reilly," Gretchen replies, her voice playful yet sincere, a hint of a coy smile dancing on her lips.

"From the instant we met, it was like something clicked—an invisible thread pulling us together. My chaotic year of enlightenment colliding with the beginning of your own journey," I say, my voice soft but charged with meaning.

"Reilly," Gretchen begins, her voice steady, yet tinged with urgency and raw emotion. "I wasn't planning to say this here, not now … but I can't keep it in any longer."

"What is it, Gretchen?" I ask, my heartbeat quickening.

She exhales shakily, then looks directly into my eyes, her gaze unwavering. "You are one of my soulmates. I know I was meant to meet you in this lifetime. You came into my life when I needed your guidance the most. And, Reilly … I've fallen in love with you," she confesses, her voice breaking slightly with vulnerability.

Before I can fully process her words, she leans in, her knee brushing against mine, the touch igniting a ripple of electricity through me. Her hands gently rise, cradling my face with an intimacy that makes the world around us fade.

And then, her lips meet mine—soft, certain, and utterly transformative. Fireworks seem to explode behind my closed eyes, vivid and wild, as though the universe itself is celebrating this moment. The hum of the West Village—the laughter, the cars, the endless buzz of life—melts away, leaving nothing but this connection, this surge of emotion, and the charged stillness between us.

I simply let myself go—into her embrace, into "us," into whatever is supposed to come next. It's not just a kiss. It's an answer, a pledge, another becoming.

I pull back for just a moment to glance at my watch, and there it is—8:06. A deep knowing settles within me as the realization takes hold: my life, in this exact moment, is right where it's meant to be.

Author's bio

Julie Tomlinson, a former advertising executive turned author, channels her lifelong passion for storytelling into compelling, heartfelt narratives that embrace vulnerability and depth. A proud later-in-life lesbian, she lives in Chicagoland with her preteen son and three spirited cats, and enjoys the endless hustle of being a devoted sports mom. As an elder Millennial, Julie fondly reflects on her generation's contributions to destigmatizing mental health and remembers the simple joys of 90s Friday Night TGIF. Fueled by early morning creativity, an energy drink (or two), and quiet, tea-filled evenings, she writes to inspire connection, spark conversation, and celebrate the power of raw authenticity. *365 Days of Becoming* is her debut novel.

 @writtenbyjt

 @julietomlinson85